TIME TRAVELERS BOOK #3

DOOMSDAY *of* TAMAS

RACE TO THE SECOND APOCALYPSE

VARUN SAYAL

Copyright © 2020 Varun Sayal
All rights reserved.

ISBN: 978-93-5437-326-8

No part of this story may be reproduced, distributed, or transmitted in any form or by any means, including photocopying, recording, or other electronic or mechanical methods, without the prior written permission of the author, except in the case of brief quotations embedded in critical articles and reviews.

This is a work of fiction. Names, characters, businesses, places, events, and incidents are either the products of the author's imagination or used in a fictitious manner. Any resemblance to actual persons, living or dead, or actual events is purely coincidental.

ABOUT
THE AUTHOR

Varun Sayal is a science fiction author who has built considerable repute in the writing world within a short period. His science fiction works, such as Time Crawlers and Demons of Time, have been phenomenal hits on Amazon, with five hundred positive reviews on Amazon and other platforms.

TABLE OF CONTENTS

1. The Phone Call 6
2. A Search Party 13
3. The UFOs 18
4. The Alien Attack 27
5. The Zombie-Mode 35
6. The Asteroid 46
7. Tamas 57
8. Hypothesis 65
9. The Return 77
10. Histor 88
11. Rigasur 99
12. Explosion 113
13. Schemer 121
14. Larem 130
15. Nark-Astra 141
16. Time Loop 147
17. Saum 155
18. Schematics 161
19. Test Run 174
20. Armageddon 188
21. Pri 193
22. Now they come for me 204
23. Abort 214
24. Warriors of Tamas 225
25. The Endgame 242

I
THE PHONE CALL

13ᵗʰ February 2074, Kolkata, India

On that clouded afternoon in Kolkata City, Moushami stepped out of her house and into the busy and cluttered produce-market called the Hatibagan Market. Her left eye-lens constantly projected her social media timeline, weather telecast, and other notifications on her retina. Every other minute, she also got a five-second feed of her toddler lying peacefully in a pram. As a single mother living without family support, this was a crucial update she'd had a technician provide for her. Her right eye lens was switched-off, as she needed it to keep an eye on the bustling street.

She loved this market. If it was up to her could spent hours moving around, buying, fish, vegetables, imitation jewelry, and condiments. She loved haggling with street vendors and getting the best deals. After her hectic days at work, it was almost therapeutic.

All the shopkeepers at Hatibagan had electronic weighing machines, smartphones, and fancy calculators now. But one thing which had not changed for the last hundred years was endless negotiations in Bangla, the local language. To the untrained eye, the noisy back-and-forth between customers and show-owners seemed like a bitter fight, but it was a routine in Hatibagan.

Almost every customer in the market had one eye preoccupied with some kind of update or notification. Some people watched a movie on their left eye, some watched news, some surfed their social media pages. Some just used it for recording the surroundings.

Moushami stopped near a fish vendor who was picking out several pomfret fish from a small freezer and laying them on a wooden table covered with a green plastic sheet.

"Ēkaṭi bhāla mācha, Boudi." – The fish is good, ma'am. The shopkeeper grinned, showing his stained, crooked teeth.

Moushami was going through the fresh produce when she heard a sharp wheezing noise above her head as if a swarm of bees was let loose. She looked up and saw two small black drones descending upon her. Each of them was fitted with a metal clasp.

She threw her stuff and ran, but the drones were too near for her to evade. Each drone clasped one of her arms. She hung between them as they started lifting her off. On-lookers gasped as she vigorously struggled mid-air, screaming for help. Many of them switched on their eye-lens cameras for recording, but a sudden sharp sound wave echoed across the market, and all the eye-lenses and mobile phones started displaying snowy-garbled screens.

Those two drones had lifted Moushami a few feet above the ground and were slowly carrying her across the market. Several people started shouting and throwing slippers, shoes, vegetables, and whatnot at the drones. A few of these objects hit the drones, but few others hit Moushami, too.

With a loud bang, and two smoke bombs landed a hundred meters apart in the market.

There was a mini stampede as people coughed and stumbled upon each other. A few men still ran behind the two drones, amidst the smoke, when a third bigger drone sharply descended. This third drone clasped a metal belt around Moushumi's waist. With the combined force of all three of them, she was lifted off with a faster velocity, taken higher up in the air, away from the market.

When the smoke settled, she had disappeared, and hundreds of people stood clueless, talking to each other. They had witnessed an abduction like never before. After a few seconds, their eye-lenses and phones were restored to normal, and they started updating their social media pages. Within the next ten minutes, the news was viral.

New Hastinapur (previously New Delhi), 1500 Kilometers away

Sameer Khanna sat in his office smoking a cigar. He was a forty-something-year-old man with a sturdy-build, greying hair, and tight jawline.

He sat on a tilted chair with his legs crossed and placed on the mahogany table. On the right side of his legs rested a small thirteen-inch laptop on which he was watching the live camera feed from the drones, wincing at every public reaction.

He was almost done watching the footage when Jadhav stormed in the room, heaving. Jadhav was the same age as Sameer but was pot-bellied and uncouth. His face sported uneven stubble, and his eyes couldn't hide his suppressed anger. He pulled a chair opposite to Sameer and sat with his head clasped in his hands and his elbows resting on the table.

"Saw the footage?" Sameer eyed him.

"What the fuck, Sameer Bhai?" Jadhav burst.

"Yeah." A cold but instinctive reply.

"If he wanted us to abduct her, then why create so much ruckus?"

Sameer sighed. He had no answer.

"And if he had to create so much noise, then why not let people record it? It went viral anyway."

"Fear of the unknown, Jadhav."

"What?"

"The moment you see something, it no longer remains scary." Sameer slowly removed his legs from the table and stood up. "Hundreds of people saw it, but there is no footage. Some people think they were drones; some may say they were UFOs. Some shitheads are even calling them flying ghosts. Confusion and panic are rapidly spreading on online forums and TV screens. It's become much bigger than it was."

"And where is that woman?"

"How should I know? He cut off the footage soon after she was lifted off. He controls the drones; we just build them."

"I don't understand."

"Neither do I. We're not supposed to."

"Yeah, we're just supposed to keep following this psychopath, this fucking hacker?" Jadhav banged the table. Sameer winced at the loud noise.

"Will you calm down? He's about to call."

Jadhav's anger turned into nervousness. He pushed back the sleeve of his sweatshirt and looked at his wristwatch. 7:04.

"And what's the significance of this 7:06? Why the same time every day?"

"How should I know?" Sameer kept the cigar aside and sat down on his chair in an attentive position. Jadhav did the same.

They both waited for the next hundred or so seconds, motionless, counting their breaths.

At exactly 07:06, the dark-net telephone app "ConTorr" buzzed with an incoming call. Thirteen different tracing software programs were immediately active on the laptop and started looking for the caller's location. Location trackers kept bouncing from one continent to the other, zeroing on a point and then again going all over the place.

"Pick up, you son-of-a-bitch," Jadhav muttered, his teeth clenched.

With trembling hand, Sameer reached out to the computer's touchscreen and pressed the green button with his index finger. The call got connected.

"Hello, boys," a half-mechanized, echoing voice boomed through the room. *"Good work with the drones. I was afraid the two would fail, but the third one took the prize."*

"I'm...I mean, we're glad you liked our work." Sameer's licked his dry lips. His throat was parched.

"Yes. I loved it. How are our bigger flying toys coming along?"

Sameer looked at Jadhav, who gave him a blank expression.

"It's on track. Components are done, need assembling. We are not sure about the software part."

"You leave the software to me. You just get the hardware ready, as per the specs sent to you."

"We will." Both of them spoke at the same time.

"Can you please release two million per day instead of one?" Jadhav blurted.

Sameer rubbed his forehead in frustration. He'd told Jadhav not to talk about money.

"Don't be greedy. Or you will lose the whole billion. All your hard-earned money will be lost in the crypto universe. It's all zeroes and ones, after all. Let your money be safe in my deeply-encrypted escrow."

Jadhav gulped.

"Now that you are in a chatty mood, I have a question. Why were you looking at the drone footage? In fact, why did you even patch the footage through your server?"

"We…we just wanted to look at how the drones are performing, so that we can make them better for you," Jadhav answered before Sameer could. He wiped the sweat off his forehead with his sleeve.

"Your elevated heartbeat and voice patterns say otherwise. I can detect when someone's lying."

Both of them sat frozen.

"I…" Sameer tried to speak, but the voice cut him off.

"I will let this one slide. Not because I am merciful, but because I have more important things to do. But don't try this again."

"Understood," Sameer quipped, like a soldier responding to his superior.

"And stop tracking me!" The voice was stern. *"Or else you will burn like this."*

The call got disconnected. Suddenly hundreds of software windows started opening up on the laptop screen. Window overlays one upon the other, several browsers, multiple tabs. Every software on the computer was activated.

Sameer and Jadhav looked at each other and panicked. Sameer tried pressing random keys, even tried to power it off, but nothing worked.

The machine overheated and crashed. Smoke emanated from between the keys.

Sameer stood frozen, while Jadhav slumped in his seat and let out a sigh.

2
A SEARCH PARTY

3362 BC, Rudrakshini's Lair, Ancient India

Rudrakshini sat on a chair made of bones and animal skin. Her already-wrinkled forehead was more crisscrossed than usual. Her eyes were open, but her thoughts took her somewhere else. A middle-aged man and a young woman stood in front of her. The man stood with his head down, while the woman looked at the man with disdain.

"I am sorry, Rudrakshini Devi…" The man blurted.

"Quiet!" Rudrakshini yelled, the candles and lamps kept around flickered and the whole room shook a little. "You only speak when you are asked to. I told you loud and clear that I need Tej because I have a critical task for which I require him. I agreed to help both of you fight that evil Nefe only because Tej gave his word that he would return the favor and help me."

"But…"

"But what? Do you mean to say that the ancient demon of time, the mighty Rigasur, is such a weakling that he cannot find another time-demon, one of his own, despite months of search? I wonder if you helped Tej defeat Nefe—or was the poor man alone in that fight? What use are your time travel powers anyway?"

"That's not fair." An indignant smile floated on Rigasur's face.

Rudrakshini turned to the woman. "What's your assessment, Pri? Can we trust this lying bastard?"

The woman wanted to speak, but Rigasur intervened. "Impossible. You are asking a new coin like her to evaluate me? I have been around for thousands of years. And by the way, I am not a lying bastard. For the past few months, I have visited more than twenty thousand massive to super-massive black holes. That's the only place Tej can be."

"Oh, don't throw these numbers and jargon at me." Rudrakshini got up in anger.

Rigasur cowered a little. Getting the queen of necromancers agitated was the last thing he wanted. "Perhaps..." He uttered in a feeble tone.

"Louder!" Rudrakshini brought her face near Rigasur's face and whispered, "I am old. Speak in a loud tone, or I won't understand a word." She walked away and again sat in her chair, still eyeing him.

"I wanted to say, if I and Pri both look together, we have a better chance. Pri is his daughter; they have a connection. It may make detection easier." Rigasur gulped.

Rudrakshini looked at Pri and then at Rigasur. "I have no problem, except I don't trust you even this much." She brought her left hand's thumb and index finger close but didn't touch them.

"I'll go, Mother." Pri turned towards Rudrakshini, folded her hands, and bowed her head. "If that helps find my father, then I will go."

"All right, Kaalpriya, you have my permission." Rudrakshini always addressed her as Kaalpriya, and not Pri. Rudrakshini found nicknames offensive. "You both are a search party then. But if anything happens to this sweet angel of mine, you will regret your very birth." She pointed at Rigasur.

Rigasur winced. He never understood Rudrakshini's love for Tej, and now for his daughter. "She is not an angel, she is a demon, a time demon," He teased.

"She is not a demon; she is an angel. You are a demon. Your actions make you an evil soul. Find Tej, and you would have repented for some of your million sins."

Rigasur drank his anger. *That's it—once we find Tej, I'm out. Away from these god-forsaken idiots.*

Pri turned to Rigasur. "I will meet you in 2077. But I need to wrap some things up there. An event is happening which requires me."

"My sources have told me that you've joined the Indian military," Rigasur chuckled. He found it amusing that a time demon was working as a government officer.

"None of your concern." Pri gave him a terse look.

"Okay. We will need to find Histor, one of the most powerful time-readers I have ever known. Your father and I worked with him the last time, and he pointed us in the right direction. Time-readers technically can't look inside black holes, but I have no other avenue left."

"Get moving, it's time for my meditation." Rudrakshini signaled with her hand.

Rigasur walked to the cement block and lay on it. He closed his eyes and was gone in a second.

Pri walked to the cement block and sat with her head down. A thousand thoughts passed through her. There were times when she kicked herself for leaving her comfy life in the future and embarking upon a search for her long-lost father. She'd visited several time readers, including Manika, but no one could find Tej. Rudrakshini had been her only support. Only because of her, Rigasur had agreed to join the search.

Rudrakshini got up and walked up to Pri. "Don't give up. Not now." She could read the girl's mind through her eyes.

"Do you think he is putting any effort?" Pri looked into her eyes.

"Who, this Rigasur? I don't trust him one bit. But let me tell you something—he is genuine in his efforts to find Tej. I am sure about that."

Pri looked up at Rudrakshini. This was the first time she'd heard her say anything good about the time demon. "Why do believe him on this? Lying is second nature to him."

Rudrakshini cachinnated. "Kiddo, I haven't whitened this hair with sunshine alone. I know how to read people and time demons. Rigasur loves Tej. However evil he is, I can sense his concern and affection for your father."

Pri smirked. "My father. Those words sound so alien to me, Rudrakshini Devi. I have a faint memory of him leaving me…" She gulped, "…forever. Since he never came back, what are the odds of finding him in the whole cosmos?" Pri's eyes were moist.

Rudrakshini looked at her with a calm demeanor. She could sense the feelings of anger and frustration in Pri. She'd grown up without her parents in a strange world, learning to use her powers and both fascinated and afraid of them.

Rudrakshini placed her fingers under Pri's chin and slowly lifted her face. She was silently sobbing.

"Tell me something. After you found yourself abandoned in the future, how did you find Manika?"

"I had a dream."

"And how did you find me?"

"The same."

"The universe wants you to find your father. And you will find him. Most of all, Tej promised to come back to me. He gave his word. So, more than anyone else, I want to get hold of that idiot."

Pri chuckled at the word "idiot" and wiped her tears. Rudrakshini's words had a magic that could pull Pri out from the deepest abyss of sadness. She again folded her hands and bowed to Rudrakshini. She laid down on the cement block and closed her eyes.

"Good girl. Always respects me before leaving. That so-called ancient demon of time has no manners." Rudrakshini muttered as she walked out of her lair, chanting.

3
THE UFOS

5th October 2077, Bengaluru, India

The control room of Special Research Group (SRG), the Indian Army, was buzzing with alarms. Situated on the seventeenth floor of a half-constructed building on the outskirts of Bengaluru city, this secretive Indian Army control room was hidden in plain sight. Though the people working in this office experienced their fair share of strange events, they were not aware that this was going to be a historic day.

Brigadier Venkatraman Sundarmurthy—or Brigadier Venkat, as he was called by his team—stood with his arms crossed, staring at two giant video screens. He stood on the upper deck while an array of army analysts scurried through the fresh images coming to them from hundreds of thousands of CCTV cameras and social-media live broadcasts.

Venkat was a man with a sleek built and the rigid posture which came with years of military service. He had thin, neatly-combed white hair, a thick white mustache, and a mole beneath the left ear. Wearing a white tee and blue denim trousers, he was sixty-two but looked only around fifty.

"Sir a news outlet has picked it up. Their headline reads, 'Two UFOs spotted on Bengaluru skyline,'" One of the analysts addressed Venkat as she adjusted her spectacles. She spoke after a pause, "Another sensationalist news channel has started a panel debate with forty-five participants. The title is 'Aliens are here'. It's going viral, sir."

"Damn these media people," Venkat cursed. "Stop focusing on the news. We can't do anything about them. Get me a better visual."

Another young analyst yelled from below, "Sir, the air force has confirmed there are no scheduled flight activities today."

"What about our partner countries? Check with US, UK, Russian, Chinese liaisons."

"Sir, China has yet to respond, but everyone else is denying intrusion in our air-space."

"Fuck," Venkat muttered. He walked down the stairs and up to a screen to take a closer look. Two faint lights were blinking a thousand kilometers up in the atmosphere.

Venkat started doling out orders. "Mathur, satellites?"

"Sir MSLV-339 will cross in seventeen minutes, but US satellite Navstar Atlantis will cross in two minutes."

"Contact them, alright? I want crystal clear pictures. I want each inch of these objects."

"Sir!"

"And someone please call Lieutenant Nancy. She should have been here."

Five kilometers away from the SRG control room, a black and orange Harley-Davidson whizzed past the cars stuck in traffic. The rider drove the bike on the broken pavement. Two traffic cops tried to stop her but in vain.

As she cleared the traffic signal and took a turn, she received a call on a radio-device plugged in her ear. She slowed down her bike and removed her helmet. Nancy was a twenty-seven-year-old with a sturdy build, a smooth face, nicely-done eyelashes, and thick lips. Pressing the button on her radio, she said, "I am on my way, sir."

"You see what's happening?" Venkat's angry voice cackled on the radio.

"Who hasn't?" She smiled as she chewed nicotine gum. "But you know Bengaluru traffic."

"Use your legs!"

"But sir, you said never to use them in public places." She bit her lower lip as she teased Venkat. She knew these were desperate times, but she enjoyed every moment.

"Yes, I said that. But these are your new orders. Get your ass here ASAP." Call disconnected.

"Yes, sir."

She pulled over her bike to one side and alighted. Unzipping her black leather jacket, she placed it on the bike. Wearing a dark red turtleneck top, black stretchable trousers, and stylish grey-black sneakers, she looked no less than a trained athlete.

Her attire, however, had a distinct peculiarity. Two thick black armbands were tied around her wrists and a thick, cylindrical tube-like belt of the same color wrapped around her waist.

She quickly tied her hair at the back of her head and secured it with a few pins. Pushing a button in the middle of her belt, she stood straight. The bands on her wrist lit up red. Thousands of nanoparticles of a synthetic chemical were being pumped through her wrist-veins into her bloodstream.

Within two seconds, the muscles in her shoulders, arms, thighs, and calves bloated a little. The skin on her face tightened, and a few green veins were visible. A menacing smile floated on her face. "Fuck yeah."

She got down, bending her left knee, touching it to the ground, her right foot firmly placed perpendicular to the road, like an Olympic racer getting into position. And then she ran at her full speed. As she ran past the vehicles stuck in traffic, she saw the numbers on her wrist-watch dial going up. She soon touched eighty kilometers per hour.

Back at the SRG headquarters, senior analyst Mathur was projecting the images he received from the US satellite on the big screen. Mathur was a bland thirty-three-year-old who fitted the description of a pot-bellied office clerk. But he was diligent and had a keen eye for detail, and, Venkat depended on him more than other analysts.

Contemporary satellite technology made it possible to view even tiny objects on the Earth's surface with remarkable accuracy. These satellites were still thousands of kilometers up in the atmosphere.

Everyone in the room stopped working for a moment and looked at the images rendering on the screen. The whole hall filled with gasps as the pictures became clear.

They were three large flying saucers, exactly as they were portrayed in the science fiction movies: plate-like circular periphery, round dome-like center. They were light green, and the sun rays reflecting on the surface indicated their metallic composition. For two of the UFOs, a think streak of red light ran around the bottom periphery of the dome where it met the vertical plate. The third UFO did not exhibit that light. It seemed inactive, though no one was sure.

"Either this is a sick joke or September fifth, 2077 is the date when this planet has their first alien contact." Venkat sat straight with his arms crossed and his hands clasping his waist. "What about the air-force?"

Mathur adjusted his spectacles as he poured into his screen "Sir, INS Sartaj is stationed near Lakshadweep. Around fifty stock-trot-33 fighters are ready to take flight from the naval ship. They can cover the distance in 9.5 minutes."

"Keep the ST-33s on standby. I have secured the necessary permissions from the Prime Minister. Being an expert in these matters, SRG will take lead on this. All other security agencies will co-operate with us."

"How did they agree to work under our command?" Mathur chuckled as he typed on his keyboard.

"Oh, it was much easier than you think." Venkat caressed his mustache. "We are the catch-all bucket for anything abnormal. Alien sightings, ghost sightings, strange occurrences; no one wants to put their hands into these things. They are ready to let SRG take the fall in case anything goes wrong."

"That's right, sir." Mathur quickly glanced at Venkat, smiled, and dug back into his screen.

There was now a wave of relaxation across the room. Having seen clear images of these objects, they now had some idea of what they were dealing with. Yes, these were aliens. Yes, this was a big deal. But it was not an unknown anymore.

"All right, team, attention." Venkat clapped loudly. "Status time." Several analysts in the room stopped working frantically and paused. Some of them peeped from behind their laptops and workstations so that they could give updates and quickly go back to work.

Venkat started a roll call.

"Ram?"

"Sir! Bengaluru airspace closed for commercial activity. All three airports have halted all outbound flights. All incoming flights are being diverted to Hyderabad and Pune."

"Good. Raashid?"

"All major tech parks in the city have been asked to evacuate. Forty-five battalions of local police and CRPF have been dispatched, each going to a major tech-park for mandating and coordinating the evacuation. Thirteen small teams of other security agencies will cover around twenty-five other major corporate establishments, including shopping centers, malls, and multiplexes. That is the extent we can cover with the available workforce. I am co-ordinating between the teams as we speak."

"What about the military? Are they securing the parameter?"

"Yes, sir. Two companies of CRPF will be stationed near the rendezvous zone. Other than that, five major entry-exit points into the city will be sealed within the next fifteen minutes by CRPF personnel, and a blockade will be established."

"Fifteen minutes, perfect. Sameer?"

"All major news channels, FM radio stations, Gramophonic influencers, and private webcasters have been mandated to repeatedly play the message we prepared. The message has been translated into Kannada, Telegu, English, and Hindi. People are advised not to panic and stay at home. All electronic billboards in the city have also suspended advertising, and are showing text with the same message."

"Great. Sujatha?"

"Emergency medical services and first responders are standby at thirty-two locations within the city. They are placed inside the emergency bunkers. But they will be on-road within three minutes SLA as required."

"All right, great job everyone, back to work. Mathur, keep studying these images and request all passing geostationary satellites to keep taking snaps. We need to monitor these objects twenty-four-seven."

Nancy entered the room and saluted. "Lieutenant Nancy Rozario reporting, sir."

Venkat turned around and responded to her salute. "At ease. Glad you could make it today." The sarcasm was not subtle.

"Apologies, sir. My boyfriend is back from Los Angeles…"

He noticed she was still wheezing, and her shirt was drenched in sweat. "After me, Room 505C."

"Sir!"

Venkat and Nancy walked to a small meeting room, where Venkat opened the door and held it open for Nancy and stepped inside behind him. This room also had a smaller TV screen, which showcased the pictures of flying saucers on a slideshow.

"Sir, I can explain."

Venkat was calm. "I am not looking for explanations. We may witness our first alien contact in the next few hours. These ships, if they are of alien origin, can react in any number of ways. I do not know what their attack will look like, or how effective our weapons will be. You and Pri may be needed in the field. I need your head in the game. I fought tooth and nail to have special individuals such as you recruited into the army. I believe, with the right intentions behind you, you and Pri can do miracles."

"We are ready, sir."

"Speaking of which, where is Pri?"

"She...ah..." Nancy stammered.

"She's ventured out of her body again. Right?" Venkat eyed Nancy. He knew she and Pri were close buddies. They both had been inducted and trained together. Being classified as special soldiers, they shared a stronger bond than others in their company.

"Yes, it's something to do with her father."

"As she told me the last time. But I need you two to drop these personal missions. You are needed here and now." Venkat poked his index finger on the metal table in between them. He had a stern expression on his face.

"Permission to speak freely, sir?"

"Yes."

"We have been with you, this SRG, for seven months now. All this time, we feel we have just been benched. My Astra-gel chemical gives me so many powers—super strength, electromagnetic induction. And Pri, she can possess anyone. She can time travel. But all we have done in these months is read previous SRG mission reports. Yes, they are interesting, but..."

"But you feel left out."

"Yes."

"Well, your bench ends today. And the action starts now. I want Pri and you ready to roll on next orders." Venkat stood up.

"Sir!" Nancy got up too and stood at attention.

"Dismissed."

Nancy walked out with a military gait. Venkat sat down and lit a cigarette. He looked at the TV screen in awe. "Aliens. Wow."

4
THE ALIEN ATTACK

Nancy entered a grey opaque metal elevator and spoke, "Barracks." A mechanical female voice responded, "Doors closing." After five seconds of sharp descent, the elevator came to a slow halt. Nancy kept tapping her foot and chewing gum until the elevator completely stopped. She hated this part, where she knew she reached her destination, but the elevator would take its own sweet time to stop moving and open the doors. As soon as the doors started moving, she adjusted herself and walked out even before the doors were fully open.

Elevator opened into a long hallway with several hundred similar blue metal doors. She walked to a door where the electronic nameplate said "Lieutenant Pri." Without knocking, she barged in.

A twenty-year-old girl sitting inside on a bed was startled. She wore a dark blue nightdress, which looked more like a casual uniform. "Doors are meant to be knocked on, Nancy." Her tone was mundane.

"And rules are meant to be broken." Nancy gave a wide smile, through which Pri could see the minced gum stuck between her teeth.

Pri made a revolted face. "Spare me the beauty of the inside of your mouth."

"On your feet, Lieutenant, our high command needs us today." Nancy slapped Pri's back, almost jolting her whole torso. She then pulled a metal chair, making as much noise as she could, and sat on it.

Pri was still shaking her head and curling her fingers into fists. "Traveling to a distant past is tough. I feel strange when I come back. It's as if I am not back." She was visibly tired.

Nancy was about to say something when a loud alarm started blaring throughout the facility. Both Nancy and Pri got up. A radio on Nancy's belt crackled with Venkat's voice. "Nancy, is Pri back?"

"Yes, sir," Nancy answered.

"Ask her to be ready and in her chamber. And you, report to the control room right now. The ships are descending." The radio went silent.

"Did he ask me to be ready in my chamber right away?" Pri had an awkward inquisitive expression on her face. "I need some time."

"Aliens, baby, aliens." Nancy chuckled as she chewed even more strongly on her gum. "Brigadier wants us in action today."

"Oh my God." Pri jumped with excitement and hugged Nancy, who clasped her arms around her and patted her back.

"Let's go."

Exactly seven minutes later, Pri had changed into her military uniform and was seated on a soft recliner chair in an empty room. On her head, she'd been fitted with a large metal helmet largely made of steel levers and electronic circuitry. This special helmet was developed for her by SRG technicians as a device that would soothe her brain quickly and enable her to move her consciousness out quickly during field missions where time was of the essence. She got comfortable and pressed a small black sphere inserted in her ear. "I am ready to roll, Brigadier, sir."

Back in the control room, Venkat responded, "Copy." He asked Mathur, "Revised ETA for the first contact?"

"Sir their trajectory has not changed, but their speed has increased. Revised ETA is 4.7 minutes. Impact location is Bhoomigaru Tech Park, West Bengaluru."

"Has it been evacuated?"

"It has seventeen buildings, sir. Evacuation is in process. The first few alarms were considered mock drills by techies."

"Idiots! Air-force status?"

"First ten of the fifty ST-33s will enter Bengaluru airspace in exactly 3.1 minutes. They won't engage first but have orders to retaliate at will. The next ten will enter after 5.2 minutes."

"Good." Brigadier touched his black earpiece. "Nancy, do you copy?"

Nancy's excited voice resounded in his ears. "Yes sir. I am on route."

"Okay, we can track you. Air Force birds will be on you in a few minutes. You are to stand by and let them engage first. You and Pri are our Plan B here."

"Noted, sir."

Venkat studied the TV screen showing the footage of rapidly descending flying saucers. They were now getting a live feed of UFOs through drone cameras flying at a few kilometers' distance from the objects. Rapid descent and high zoom shook the video.

"Mathur, keep monitoring the frequencies. Though they don't look like they're in a mood to talk."

"Sir, what if the aliens communicate on frequencies that we can't even capture? What if they are using quantum tunneling to send messages?"

Venkat frowned. Not only did he disparage Mathur's use of jargon, but he also despised his speculations, especially at this crucial stage. But given the kind of threats his team usually handled, he often encouraged random ideation—however stupid it sounded.

"No time for these theories, Mathur; we are in the field. We must deal with this here and now. Just wait, watch, and react."

Mathur gulped.

Bhoomigaru Tech Park was in complete chaos. Several vehicles were trying to leave at once and were stuck on the road. Bengaluru airspace was declared a no-flight zone, and hence no flying-vehicle-based evacuation was possible. While a lot of employees working there had decided to leave, several others had gone inside the underground basement parking lots and hidden wherever possible.

The UFOs had now aligned themselves in a V-shape flying formation, with two of them flying a little higher above the third one in the middle. They were descending with higher acceleration, and their menacing shadows now cast themselves on the buildings and vehicles beneath. A strange buzzing sound emanated from within them, which was much different from an aircraft's fly-by sound.

On the ground, people stuck in the vehicles now started alighting and running away in panic, stampeding. Hundreds of men and women still wearing their tech-park badges and carrying laptop bags, stumbled upon each other and the vehicles between them.

Ten ST-33 Indian air-force fighter aircraft were visible at a distance, thundering throughout the area. They broke into three formations of four, three, and three, each targeting one UFO.

UFOs were barely a few hundred feet above the tech-park when one of them fired. A rectangular red blast of plasma energy emanated from beneath the UFO and struck one of the buildings in the tech park, causing an immediate explosion. Concrete, steel, and glasses were ruptured and thrown out as the whole building experienced a shockwave. Tonnes of heavy debris landed on the people and parked vehicles, below crushing them instantly. The building was in flames.

The first shots had been fired, and the ST-33s were now green to fire at will. ST-33s were extremely lightweight aircraft, but lethal fighters. Each was equipped with short-range missiles and heavy artillery guns. Their armor was light, but their swift maneuvers helped boost their defense.

The UFOs broke formation, taking multiple fly-bys over the tech park. They now started firing openly on all the seventeen buildings. Within a few seconds, the whole cluster of skyscrapers was in flames. The first building had developed huge cracks and was about to come down like a pack of cards.

The situation on the ground was chaotic, the environment filled with smoke, dust, and people's screams. Many crushed under the debris were partially hurt and stuck and called for help. Two teams of CRPF commandos rapidly fired on the UFOs, using their automatic machine guns, but the bullets just ricocheted off the ship-bodies.

Soon, the ST-33s also engaged, and each of them fired one thermal radiation missile at the UFOs, which they skillfully avoided. Two of the missiles crashed into the buildings in the tech park. The UFOs shot back and took down two fighters. Since this was a full-fledged air-battle, Venkat asked the on-ground forces to first help the civilians, then leave the area.

Within two minutes, ten more ST-33s entered the scene, and the whole area became an open battlefield. The area within five kilometers around Bhoomigaru was now a death-zone. Anyone on the ground or in nearby buildings was doomed, missiles and plasma ray shots zapping back and forth over the next few minutes.

Two minutes into the battle, things were not looking good for the ST-33 fighters. Five had been shot down, and none of their missiles had hit the UFOs. Artillery fire was a waste, the UFO was armor too resilient for it.

Back in the control room, Venkat was fighting with his superiors. "No, sir, believe me. My special soldiers can handle these fucking aliens….yes, they can do what the fighter-jets can't…please recall them. The whole city will be destroyed, sir. All those lives are on your conscience."

Venkat relayed the footage of five ST-33 fighters going down and finally got a go-ahead. He disconnected his call, then immediately radioed his team B. "Nancy, Pri, the fighter planes are pulling out. You are good to go. Now listen to me carefully. Pri, you go possess an alien in one of the ships. Figure out what's happening."

Pri closed her eyes and started to concentrate. She had very recently learned to use her skills. Finding destinations was difficult for her. Her current body was her anchor, and she was looking for destinations—any living organisms inside those alien ships.

Venkat addressed his other soldier. "Nancy, throw a few objects on these ships. Get their attention."

"You sure, sir? Artillery hasn't worked on them." Nancy's panting voice came through. She was running around the tech park, trying to find the right place to draw the ships in. The ships were still hovering over the area and demolishing the remnants of the building.

"Yes, I am." Venkat was stern. "I have a plan; just bear with me for now." He was making a tough call, an unpopular choice—asking the fighter planes to leave and moving his special-individuals team in. But his gut was telling him he was right. His primary task was to over-power these alien ships. But not at the cost of a whole city.

"ST-33s are moving out, sir." Mathur looked up from his monitor, perplexed. He wasn't sure why this was a good move.

Nancy now stood at the western periphery of the tech-park near the main gate. She stood amidst hundreds of empty deserted vehicles, mostly cars, and scooters.

"I think I am in a good position, sir."

"All right, power-up."

"With pleasure." Nancy grinned and hit the red button in the middle of her belt. More chemicals were pumped into her bloodstream. Her pupils dilated, her muscles bulged. Small green veins were visible on her forehead, down to her cheeks. A few sparks of electricity went through her body. Her whole body was now a powerful electro-magnet, the intensity and magnetic field of which she could control with her brain.

She looked at a car parked nearby and waved her hand at it. The car shook a little. She curled the fingers of her right hand into a fist and moved her arm high up in the air. The car started rising in the air as if an invisible force were lifting it.

Nancy swung her arm as if throwing something in the air, and the car flew several hundred meters. It kept following the parabolic trajectory until smashed itself into one of the UFOs and exploded.

"Woohoo!" Nancy jumped like a kid.

Venkat stood quiet for a moment, carefully considering the screen in front of him. The UFO that had been hit was no longer moving. It stood in the air. The streak of light cycling its periphery sped up.

He yelled, "It's going to fire, Nancy!"

5
THE ZOMBIE-MODE

The next instant, a plasma ray shot from beneath the UFO. Had Nancy not leaped a few feet to her left, she would have been incinerated. Instead, three cars behind her went up into flames.

Nancy's heart was racing, and she felt angry. "Bring it on, you motherfucking aliens." She curled up both her fists and pulled two cars with all her might. She swung both towards the UFO.

The UFO blasted the cars in the air before it hit them and paced towards Nancy. Nancy started picking the cars one by one and threw them towards the UFO. The UFO came down, blasting plasma rays, and flew a few feet above Nancy, crossing the street and blasting several vehicles. It shot up a few hundred feet in the air, returning for a second pass.

Pri, on the other hand, was facing a weird situation. She opened her eyes, and nothing she saw was making sense. She was inside the body of the alien flying the UFO. She sat in a small dark room on a rigid seat. It seemed as if her body was part of the seat, and not separate from it. A big console, full of hundreds of buttons and levers, stared her in the face. There was no screen to look at. She looked at her host's hands, arms, torso, and rest of the body wherever the skin was not covered in cloth and armor. It was all dark green and red, with reptilian scales. She touched her face and it felt wet with a gooey liquid, which sent an eerie sensation down her body. *What the hell is this alien?*

She searched for memories and thoughts in the alien's brain, but there were none. It only had the basic know-how of flying this ship—as if the brain had been blanked out. She took full control of the alien's mobility.

Time travel and human possession were new to Pri. She learned about her powers a few years back but rarely used them. Even human possession was not easy for her, and this alien's brain was remarkably different. Being inside it was far too taxing for her.

But she remembered what Brigadier told her before she left her anchor. "Pit them against each other." That's what she sought to do, then get out quickly. She gave another careful look to the console, and one part of it brought a smile to her lips—if this alien had lips; she was not sure. One part of the console had a small black navigation dark screen on which two moving dots were visible. *These must be the two other ships.*

On the ground, things were not easy for Nancy. She had hurled more than seventy vehicles at the UFO, but its surface bore no scratch. In many instances, she barely saved herself from the plasma ray shots targeted at her. "If you are up to something, Brigadier sir right now would be the time. I feel I'm running out of my juice." Her voice sounded exhausted.

Before Venkat could say anything, he saw something strange on the screen. The other two UFOs started fighting with each other. They rose higher and higher in the air until one of the UFOs sped towards the other and smashed into it. That caused a visible impact on both the objects, their peripheries corroding and set on fire.

Why would aliens engage with each other all of the sudden?
"Yes!" Venkat clenched his teeth. "Pri did it." He saw something on the footage which caught his attention. He ran over to Mathur's desk. "Play the previous footage for me."

"The one where they smashed into each other?"

"Just after that."

"Here it is."

"Zoom in."

The image was pixelated a little but revealed the smoke, fire, and a dent in the UFO periphery. A strong hit from the same material as the UFOs were made from could destroy it. A subtle smile floated across Venkat's face.

Inside the UFO, Pri was joyous too, but she felt she could not possess the alien any longer. She planned one more smash and then bailing out. But she could not take it anymore and left the body.

She woke up in her anchor body back at the SRG facility. Her head was spinning. She immediately got up from her seat and vomited in a corner. When she could catch her breath, she rested her back against a wall and sat with her eyes closed. She then spoke on her comms. "Sir, I couldn't stay any longer. I am out. And I am in no position to go back."

"Don't worry. You did the right thing. I know how to get these sons of bitches." Venkat addressed Mathur. "Send a medical team to where Pri is."

Mathur nodded.

Venkat thought for a moment, then spoke to Nancy. "Nancy, stop hurling vehicles at them."

Nancy, who had lifted a huge truck seven feet up in the air and was trying to balance it in mid-air using both her hands, yelled, "What now, sir?"

"Forget cars and trucks. You need to hurl one UFO at the other."

"What?" Nancy let go of the truck, and it came crashing down on the cars beneath with a loud bang. She ran towards a corner and took shelter behind a series of five charred vehicles pelted upon each other. "The induction field needed for me to control such a huge UFO…I mean, I would need full-power configuration zombie mode for that. And we won't have control of what happens after that."

Venkat took a deep breath. "Listen. I know what I am asking of you is too much. But believe me, that's the only way. When you go to zombie mode, you will be fully cognizant for fifteen seconds. Use this time well."

"And after that?"

"We'll see."

Beads of perspiration appeared on Nancy's forehead. "Sir. But after those fifteen seconds, I may…"

"Just do it, Nancy, it's an order," Venkat cut her off. In the heat of the ongoing conflict, he had given the orders but felt a momentary feeling of dread run deep down his spine.

Nancy clenched her teeth. "Yes, sir." She stood up and patted her chest. "It's gonna be fine." She knew zombie mode was insanity. But she also knew Venkat wouldn't order it unless required.

She walked to the center of the street, amongst the mess of iron, rubber, and vehicle parts. The UFO was racing towards her, shooting the plasma rays. The other two UFOs were no longer smashing into each other and stood in the air without much movement. Large chunks of their peripheries were damaged, and smoke and fire were visible.

Without wasting an instant, Nancy pressed the button in the middle of her belt, and this time, turned a lever clockwise. A huge charge of electricity ran through her body. Her muscles bulged, even more, tearing her uniform. Her facial skin turned grey, her lips puffed up, and drool fell between them. Green cracks on her face deepened.

"Death to you motherfuckers!" her voice went hoarse.

The UFO passed above, targeting the blasts at her, but she jumped like an acrobat and evaded most of them. Just as the flying saucer crossed her, she concentrated her magnetic field at it. She could feel the huge chunk of metal flying away from her and slowing down. The several-ton heavy flying saucer was now in her control. It could only rise a few feet above in the air and now stood shaking. Without wasting a breath, Nancy swayed her hands and whole torso sideways. The UFO moved like the stone tied at the end of a slingshot and crashed into a nearby building, breaking concrete, steel rails, and windows.

The other two UFOs, engulfed in flames, now raced towards her, in close formation. Nancy pulled the one in her control out of the building, bringing a lot of debris with it, which came down on the ground crashing. She flung it towards the two incoming UFOs. The flying saucer sped like a frisbee. Both of the incoming ones took a sharp oblique turn, and one of them managed to avoid the collision completely, but the other one collided head-on. A huge explosion resulted, the waves of which swept the whole area.

Nancy could not stay standing and was thrown several feet away like a rag doll.

But she stood up the next instant. Fifteen seconds were over. She was no longer in control of herself.

Both the affected UFOs were now in tatters, with their external armor ruptured and wiring and equipment dangling out. One of them flew half a mile and collapsed in the middle of the construction site. The other one scratched on the side of a nearby building, drawing sparks and flames as its metal body rubbed against the concrete, further damaging it. It finally crashed onto a nearby highway, where it kept tumbling through the highway street lamps before the friction with the asphalt of the road brought it to a complete stop.

Back in the control room, everyone let out a cheer of joy. Analysts hugged each other, and others banged their tables. Two of the three threats had been brought down. Venkat still stood in a pensive pose. They had secured a small win, but the battle was far from over.

The third UFO was already dented with previous impacts but was semi-functional. Half of it was on fire, but it could still fly low and send down intermittent plasma ray blasts. It flew towards Nancy at a sharp velocity, but this time, Nancy stood her ground. She was flexing her shoulder and neck muscles and had a wicked smile on her face. A white froth dripped onto her chin and neck. There was no fear or anger in her eyes. There was only insanity.

As the UFO dashed for Nancy, she stretched out her arms and sought control over the giant metal body. The flying saucer was not trying to hit her with plasma rays but was intending a physical collision. The outmost periphery of the UFO came to a sudden halt just within inches of where Nancy was standing. Her palms were almost touching the far end of the UFO. The gigantic ship stood there, floating in the air, tilted at an angle where Nancy stood with her arms stretched out and her left leg pulled back with her right foot firmly in place. Near her body, her magnetic field was the most powerful. "You are not going anywhere."

She swung her whole body 360 degrees. The UFO was thrown across the street, until it crashed into the lowermost level of a multi-level parking lot, demolishing it instantly. With a series of huge explosions, all the upper levels, along with their parked vehicles, came crashing upon the UFO one by one.

Back in the control room, there was a momentary pause, and then the whole room erupted into joy.

Venkat, too, let out a faint smile. That was the most he allowed himself to be happy. Hundreds of lives had been lost, and several buildings destroyed, but a hard-fought battle was finally over. They prevented a whole city from being leveled.

Mathur ran towards Venkat and gave him an awkward hug, which he did not like one bit, but he patted Mathur's back a few times. "Enough, kid."

Mathur left Venkat and went back to his seat.

Venkat had to yell to drown all their voices. "All right, guys, a big round of applause for Nancy and Pri, our warriors on the ground. They deserve real praise."

The whole hall burst into claps and cheers.

Venkat smiled, then spoke on his radio. "Well done, Nancy. You have saved the day and countless lives."

The voice on the other end was menacing. "Who is Nancy? I am coming to get you."

Venkat's facial expression froze, and he gulped. The radio line was disconnected. "Mathur...MATHUR!" His scream brought the whole room to silence.

Mathur looked shocked. "What happened...sir?"

"Nancy is out of control. Track her, right now."

Mathur sat back on his workstation and started clacking his keyboard. He looked up. "Sir, her GPS dot is moving very fast."

"Run your trajectory algorithms. Where's she going?"

"Here," Mathur gulped.

Ten minutes had passed. Venkat's brain was racing fast. Nancy had got into zombie mode three months back, too. It had happened by mistake during a training exercise, when a huge blow on her belt button oozed more chemicals than required into her. She ended up seriously wounding forty other cadets, of which seven hadn't recovered for a few weeks, and two were paralyzed for life. At that time, multiple shots of sonic waves from three large military amplifiers were the only thing that calmed her down enough for them to take her into custody.

Doctors later powered her down with heavy sedatives and modified her belt to have a small lever for zombie-mode activation.

But this time, they were in the city and just reeling from a major alien attack. Military equipment was far away.

"Sir, she is closing in." Mathur's shaking voice broke Venkat's chain of thoughts. The conflict that just wrapped up had exhausted him. He sank into his chair, waiting for what was coming for him. But then he looked at the fearful faces of analysts, all of them looking at him. *No, I can't give up. It's not only my life at stake here.*

He got up with resolve and ran over to the weapons cabinet. "Everyone! Grab a weapon." He took out a Styger Blitz X-22 rifle, stepped aside, and started loading it.

There was a muffled explosion at the entrance, and everybody in the room looked in that direction. It was followed by the sound of gunfire. Nancy was here.

Venkat paused for a second and resumed readying himself for combat. All the analysts stumbled and ran towers the cabinet. They started taking out whichever guns and pistols they could get their hands on.

When Venkat was inserting a magazine into the gun, a sudden serendipitous thought stuck him. "Why the hell did I not think of this before?" he murmured to himself. He looked around and licked his parched lips. "Who can tell me where Pri is?"

"She's in the med bay," reported Sujatha, one of the analysts.

"Get her on comms."

"But sir…"

"Now!"

Ten seconds later Venkat was arguing with the nurse-lieutenant over the radio. "It's an order, Aqsa. Wake Lieutenant Pri up, now!"

"Sir we have given her sedatives. Her head was spinning."

"Give her adrenaline, give her something! Lives are at stake here. Wake her up and put her on comms."

He could hear some commotion on the radio, and then he heard Pri's feeble voice. "Sir. Pri this side." The nurse-lieutenant Aqsa had stabbed an adrenaline injection in her thigh, and she was weak but awake.

Venkat knew Pri was weak, but time was running out. "Pri, I need you to concentrate. Nancy is out of control."

"How, sir?"

"Zombie mode." Venkat heard the sound of more gunfire, this time closer.

"What can I do here?"

"Possess her."

"What?" Pri never thought she would be asked to possess her friend.

"Yes. Do it. If you possess her, you will control her mind, not the chemicals inside her."

There was a loud bang on the control room entrance, and the metal door came crashing down. All the analysts in the room now faced the door with their arms stretched out and the grasp on their guns tightened.

The smoke cleared, and the bulky figure of Nancy appeared. In addition to the zombie-mode changes in her body, she also had bullet holes in multiple places in her body, where the blood had dried out. She was unrecognizable.

"Where the hell is Mr. Brigadier?" Nancy hissed. She was only a few feet away from them.

"Hold your fire, everyone. She is one of us." Venkat slowly walked from between the analysts and came to the front. His X-22 was fully loaded, and the safety was off, but he was not pointing it at her. "Nancy, this is not you. Calm yourself down."

"I warned you, Brig, but you still went ahead. You saved the world from them. But how will you save yourself from me?" A thick froth dripped from Nancy's mouth.

Before Venkat could say something, Nancy dashed towards him. He and few others fired, but in a split second, she had her hands on Venkat's neck and had lifted him two feet up in the air, as if he was a light mannequin.

Venkat dropped his gun and clasped Nancy's muscular arms, but her grasp was herculean. He gasped for his breath and shook violently. She hung him in the air between herself and the analysts so that no one has a clear shot.

"L…Let him go, Nancy, or we will shoot." Mathur mustered courage.

Nancy tilted her neck and peeped from behind Venkat. "Go, ahead, shoot. After I am done with him, you are next."

Mathur's forehead was drenched in sweat. He stood frozen. They all did. They had periodic gun training, but they were not soldiers. This was not a clean shot, and they all hesitated, all afraid for their lives.

Venkat's struggles had turned feeble as his face turned violet and his eyes widened. There was a sudden pink glow in Nancy's eyes, and she let go of Venkat. He fell on the floor, not moving.

All the analysts were now even tenser as Nancy stared at them with a wide grin.

6
THE ASTEROID

स‍स‍स‍स‍स‍स‍स‍स‍स‍स‍स‍स‍स‍

As seconds passed, her grin slowly vanished. Her head straightened, and her posture also lightened. After a few seconds, she finally spoke. "Hold your fire. It's me. Pri. I am in control. I am putting her to sleep. Take them to the med-bay." Nancy collapsed on the ground, unconscious.

Everyone waited for a few seconds, and then Mathur ran towards Venkat. He checked the brigadier's pulse. He turned back in tears. "He's alive. Can someone give me a hand?"

6th October 2077, New Hastinapur, India

Sameer and Jadhav sat in the same room, their eyes on the laptop in front of them. The time was 7:03 PM. They had been sitting quietly for the last ten minutes. Jadhav had been rubbing his jaw and tapping his foot, while Sameer had been smoking a cigar and occasionally checking his laptop, making sure the internet connection was smooth and running. They would not want to miss the call.

"What have we become?" Jadhav muttered in anger.

"Survivors." Sameer's tone was nonchalant as he puffed out a ring of smoke.

Jadhav was indignant. "You don't feel a thing, Sameer Bhai. Right? Hundreds of people were killed in Bengaluru. Billions of rupees worth of property destroyed. All because of us. What have we done?"

"Not now, Jadhav." Sameer was irate. "My only goal in life is to stay alive. Stay breathing for one more day. Whoever this person is, he is unforgiving. When he can mercilessly kill hundreds, then both of us are just a drop in the ocean. I want to stay safe, get all my money back, secure it, and then perhaps we will take care of this bastard."

Jadhav sat quiet, but still nervously tapped his foot.

At exactly 7:16, the Contorr app buzzed with an incoming call. No tracking software ran in the background this time. Sameer looked at Jadhav. "Don't say anything foolish." He pressed his lips as if anticipating an answer. The call-tone ran in the background.

Jadhav nodded reluctantly.

Sameer went ahead and clicked the green "Receive" button.

"Hello, Boys. How are you doing? Wait, keep the answers to this question to yourself." The menacing voice of the unknown hacker buzzed through the computer and echoed in the room.

"Shall we now consider our contract complete?" Sameer calculated his words and balanced his tone. He did not want to sound too aggressive, but not too meek either.

"Absolutely. You had to deliver three robotic solutions. You delivered all three. The contract is considered complete. I will shortly transfer all your funds back into your crypto-wallets."

"Great. It was good working with you," Sameer said with a feeble fake smile, hoping the call would disconnect and all their problems will go away.

"That was a great fireworks show yesterday." Jadhav let out a nervous laugh.

Sameer eyed him with anger. Why the hell was that comment needed?

"Thanks, Jadhav. During these past few months, I feel we three have come quite close. As if we are brothers."

Sameer smirked at the word "brothers." He felt more like a slave to a mad master.

The voice continued, *"I feel obligated to share some personal details with you. My name is Tamas. A resident of the world of zeroes and ones. Eternally swimming in the ocean of electrical pulses powering your motherboards."*

"Why are you telling us about yourself?" Sameer did not like where this was going. He wanted them to part quickly.

"Well, we will never see each other again, that's why." The voice sounded sad. *"And Jadhav, if you liked that show, you are going to love what's about to happen."*

"What's about to happen?" Sameer sat up in his chair. His heartbeat went up.

Jadhav froze as well.

"A mini fireworks-show at your premises."

The gunfire came across the distance and both Sameer and Jadhav were on their toes.

"What is the meaning of this?" Sameer shouted at the laptop. "We did what you said. We worked hard and built each technology component you asked for. Now you keep your word, goddammit!"

"I am not obligated by codes and contracts of moral behavior. Our contract is over, and I can't leave any…how do you say it poetically…loose ends."

Sameer drew his pistol from underneath his jacket. Jadhav ran to a corner, picked up a large automatic rifle, and loaded it.

"If I ever leave this place alive, I am going to find you and strangle you with my own bare hands." Sameer was fuming with anger.

"That's a noticeably big if. And even if you do, I am nowhere to be found. Distributed over millions of computing systems, I am at no single place. I am everywhere."

There was a loud bang outside, and they both now pointed their guns at the door. Suddenly, the wall behind them collapsed with a mini-blast and two small black drones emerged from the smoke. Each had four small rotors attached at the end of four arms, floating. In the middle was an automatic pistol soldered to the metallic drone body. The trigger was rigged with wires going to a battery system attached below the pistol.

Sameer made a last-ditch attempt. "Look, Tamas. Let us go. Okay. You can keep our money."

"Money? That holds no worth for me. It is all zeroes and ones. I can create it at will and destroy it at will."

Jadhav did his bit. "We two are not alone. Thousands of workers worked on the machines we made for you."

"They were all worker bees. You two are the queens. And today I take the queens. May your final journey be as horrible as your death is going to be. May you both rest in pieces."

Sameer and Jadhav shared a glance. Jadhav saw a light red shining dot on Sameer's forehead. But before his reaction time made him realize what the dot was, both the drones shot simultaneously. Two bullets fired: one landed in Jadhav's heart, the other in Sameer's forehead, and they collapsed on the ground.

Small boxes from below each of the drones opened, and two tiny, sealed packets of cocaine fell on the ground. The drones flew out.

The laptop's telephony app shutdown and a lot of small black software windows started opening on the laptop. All the folders on the laptop were being remotely accessed, and the files, call logs, and internet activity was being deleted. Within seconds, the whole disc was wiped clean. Afterward, the telephony app was installed again and started making calls out to darknet IPs of known drug dealers in the area. Any incoming police investigator would see this as a drug conflict and would be led down a rabbit hole of dead ends.

8th October 2077, Army Infirmary, SRG headquarters, Bengaluru

Thirty-six hours since the alien attack was over, and the whole city was reeling from death and destruction. Venkat, who initially was thought to have slipped into a coma, opened his eyes. He lay on the infirmary bed with a large pad wound around his neck to keep it stable. Manual strangulation had caused damage to his cervical vertebrae, but the larynx was unharmed.

The upper part of his bed had been pulled up at forty-five degrees to bring him to a sitting posture. Three different life-sign monitors were connected to veins in his arm and the back of his hand. He spoke feebly with medical staff and often smiled.

Nancy and Pri entered the room and stood next to his bed. Nancy had a few bandages on her face, neck, and arms, and wore a hospital gown. She also used an adjustable elbow-support crutch to walk and support her body weight.

Pri looked all right and was dressed in a white shirt and dark brown trousers, her hair tied neatly at the back.

Venkat smiled when he saw them and tried to adjust himself up the bed, but could not. "I guess I didn't practice enough chokeholds during our Krav Maga sessions."

Pri gave a customary smile, but Nancy stood with her head down, drowning in guilt.

Venkat looked at Nancy and chuckled. "Look at you, just a few bandages. I wish I had your super-healing abilities."

Nancy wiped a tear. "I am sorry, sir." Her throat was heavy.

"Oh, shut up. It wasn't you who went all Godzilla on me. It was the zombie inside of you. And remember, it was me who ordered you to go full nuts."

"I still can't shake those memories, sir. I will never activate that mode again."

"Don't you say that." Venkat was stern. "You saved this city and millions of lives. Yes, there were collateral damages, but because of you two, many men, women, and children are breathing today. Don't forget that."

Both women nodded.

"We will let you rest." Pri smiled and pressed Venkat's hand.

Nancy stood with her head down.

Venkat looked at her. "Nancy. Look at me."

Nancy looked up. Her face was red, and tears were streaking down her face. "Sir!"

"Stop crying."

She wiped her tears and stood straight.

"Get back in shape quickly. And be ready, both of you. I have a strong feeling this is not over yet. Do you hear me?"

"Yes, sir!" both quipped together in a military tone as their postures tightened.

Pri hesitated for a moment and then spoke. "Sir, I need to venture out again. It's regarding my…"

"Your father. I know, Nancy told me. Go on, do your thing. Family is important, too. But keep checking back."

"Sure, sir. I can only report back every ten hours. I can never come back to the same moment. That's the maximum accuracy I can hit while time-traveling."

Venkat took a deep breath and looked in the oblivion. "Damn, I don't even claim to understand this time travel stuff. But be careful with it. Many in our government haven't ever met a time traveler or a super-soldier." He looked at Nancy. "Many are afraid of your powers, and many others want to use it for their material benefit. And your participation in this operation will bring more attention to both of you, and more pressure on me."

"Pressure for what sir?" A look of concern appeared on Pri and Nancy's face.

"Frankly, I don't know yet." He paused and looked at them. "You know what, don't think about it right now. Pri, go find your father. Nancy, get some rest and get well. Dismissed."

They both reacted with a military salute and then slowly walked out. Venkat closed his eyes.

28th August 2077, Astronav-23 Space Observatory
7,000 miles above the Earth's surface

Astronav-23 was a fifty-year-old four thousand pound space observatory orbiting the Earth with a seventy-two-hour orbital period. Along with PSLV-XXIV, it was the second dedicated multi-wavelength space telescope launched by India in the year 2026.

It had been fully functional all these years, with a focus on near-Earth-asteroids, NEAs. It kept relaying NEA data to two major monitoring stations on Earth: one in Chennai, India, and one in Sacramento, the United States.

Down at an empty office at fifty-fourth Avenue, Sacramento City, monitoring operator Hafisa Zubair was sipping her evening coffee. It was 6:44 PM local time, and she was wrapping up her report on a possible new asteroid which Astronav-23 had identified a couple of hours back.

She received a call on her cell-phone, a smiling picture of her fiancé Aijaaz displayed on the phone screen. She loved the dimples on his cheeks and the carefully-designed stubble he always maintained. She quickly got up and briskly walked to a dedicated phone room. As soon as she entered, she swiped the green button.

"Hello, *Mohtarma*." Aijaaz's hoarse voice echoed in the room, the voice she fell in love with during those long phone conversations. She waited the whole day for him to call her *Mohtarma*, Urdu for madame.

"Hello, *Huzur*." She chuckled. "What happened? Can't you wait to see me?"

Aijaaz laughed. "I am all right, love. But someone else in this house just can't stay without seeing Mommy." His voice went several notches down, talking to someone else in the room. "Jannat, you want to talk to Mommy?"

"Put her on video, Aijaaz." Hafisa's smile widened. She so wanted to go back home and cuddle her three-year-old daughter, Jannat. Hafisa switched to a video call, and a shaky video of an innocent face appeared. Sitting in her father's lap, the cute kid with chubby cheeks was chewing a toy between her teeth.

"What is my darling doing?"

"Eating everything non-edible." Aijaaz's face was half-visible as he focused his phone on Jannat.

"When are you coming, Mommy?" Her soft voice was music to Hafisa's ears.

"Mommy will be late today. Be a good girl."

After a fifteen-minute conversation, Hafisa came back to her desk, a faint smile still floating on her lips. In front of her was a set of two seventeen-inch computer screens, on one of which she was looking at faint asteroid images. She zoomed in on one of the images until she could see the asteroid surface with clarity. She then dragged the image and pushed it into an empty window on the second screen, where an image recognition software started drawing point to point vectors across the image.

The software then started matching the vector-map with several other documented asteroids. Multiple colorful images started appearing and vanishing in a small square box at the bottom left as software quickly generated match scores with them. A match score of more than eighty-five percent indicated that the asteroid was the same as one previously seen.

Hafisa was at the edge of her seat the whole time, looking at the software doing its job while taking small sips of her coffee. On the other screen, the faint image of a huge rock with gigantic discernible craters was frozen. This asteroid was previously unseen but was now emerging from behind Neptune when the space-telescope snapped its pictures.

The software finally came to a halt. *Total Number of matches found: Zero.*

Hafisa jumped in her seat and could not keep herself from giggling with joy. Her wide grins showed her braces. Not every day did a monitoring operator find a new asteroid. Hafisa picked up her cell phone and almost dialed her colleague Sridhar in Chennai, but then she consulted her watch and halted. Sridhar's shift was not to begin until the next two hours.

She powered up another desktop system and started preparing for a video log. Although all the readings taken by Astronav-23 were automatically recorded and sent to a secure server, the managers still encouraged the monitoring operators to regularly video log their work.

As she clicked on her keyboard, her tired yet happy face was visible on the webcam. She took a couple of wet tissues and rubbed the oily skin below her eyebrows and around her nose. After adjusting her headscarf and the collars of her shirt, she assumed a plastic smile and pressed the record button. A red blinking sign of REC along with a large red dot appeared on the top right. An increasing timer, which began at 00:00:00, was also displayed.

"I am Hafisa Zubair, monitoring operator at Sacramento station. Today at exactly 4:37 PM Pacific, the space observatory Astrosat-23 started relaying pictures of a previously unknown asteroid. For the record, the software has assigned it the name…" Hafisa read verbatim from the other screen, "... 2077-NEA-511. The estimated weight is 82 billion kilograms, the estimated diameter is 1.3 kilometers." Hafisa kept speaking as she saw these details on the other screen. "Ideally, the space telescope would have taken the pictures of rock of this size entering the solar system a few months back. But we are only seeing it today, as it has appeared from behind Neptune's shadow and is traveling towards the center of the Solar System."

Hafisa paused for a second as the software now started showing the projected trajectory and related metrics. "Software estimates a one-in-two hundred chance of collision with Earth." Hafisa paused and gulped. She continued as she realized the video was still recording. "According to current velocity and distance measurements, the estimated time to collision is 1022 days, 16 hours, and 59 minutes. A 99% confidence interval was applied. Date of impact, June 16th, 2080. The software classifies it as a Potentially Hazardous Asteroid, PHA class seven."

Hafisa paused the video log and clicked on the finish button. The video screen disappeared, and the movie file was saved on the system in one of the folders. Hafisa slowly sank back in her chair. Any signs of a smile on her face had disappeared. Her throat felt parched, and she felt weak in her gut.

She was no astrophysicist, but she knew what this meant. Collision-odds as low as one in ten thousand were damning enough to concern astrophysicists. Odds of one in two hundred meant a sure-shot impact event. A mega-asteroid was on collision course with Earth, and they had less than a thousand days.

7
TAMAS

༺༻༺༻༺༻✥༺༻༺༻༺༻

Hafisa quickly collected all her stuff in her large purse and stepped out of the office building. Sun had set on Sacramento sky more than half an hour ago, and streets were lit with dim low-power lampposts. The office district was usually this empty by 6 PM.

For the fifth time, she tried the number of Mariela Garcia, deputy director of the Astronav-23 program, but the phone again went to voicemail. This was too big to leave for the next day. She had been trying to contact several top officers on their numbers, but none of them responded.

She even tried to text Mariela, but her texts were failing to deliver. And the texts she sent a few minutes back to Aijaaz were also showing failed delivery. "Stupid phone companies. Their networks are always overloaded," she cursed under her breath.

Finally, Hafisa fired up the taxi app. On usual evenings, she walked half a mile to the corner of the next street from where an electric bus took her directly to her home in the suburbs. The bus service was free of charge.

But today was different. Today she needed to meet Maria at any cost. *If she's not picking the phone, I'll hit her door,* she had decided.

Within ten seconds, she got a cab-match. A tiny yellow-painted flying taxi slowly descended at a designated spot near her. It was a small two-seater cabin, with two giant horizontally aligned rotors in front and a vertical sleek rotor at back. She had sat in these only once when her father had suffered cardiac arrest and she had to rush behind the emergency-flying vehicle to the hospital. They were damn expensive.

She sat inside, and immediately the automated seat belt clasped around her torso.

The soft, soothing voice of the taxi-operating AI echoed inside the small chamber. "Welcome, Miss Zubair. Hope you are doing good this evening." The taxi app had recognized her using facial recognition. "Where do you wish to go today?"

"House number 639, sub-plot B, 23rd Avenue."

"Very well. Your estimated fare is $749. Do you accept the charges?"

Hafisa reacted as if she was stung by a bee, but she was already stung enough with what she had seen on her computer screen today. "$749 for less than five miles?"

"Sorry, I didn't understand. Do you accept the charges?"

"I do." She planned to reimburse every dollar later from the company expense allowance.

Rotors started churning, and the taxi slowly began to rise. It lifted off to fifty feet and then entered the air traffic control-designated flying pathway.

Hafisa sat with her eyes closed when a notification sound on her phone broke her chain of thoughts. She looked at her phone, where a short text appeared on the screen. Her phone's download folder was automatically opened, and all previous downloads had been wiped off. Only one file was visible; it was titled PlayMe.dlk. Hafisa hesitated for a moment and then clicked it.

"Hello, Hafisa. Good Evening. My name is Tamas. I am sorry I could not make a direct call to you, as these networks are monitored. But this file is an interactive system with a million pre-filled conversational responses."

"What is the meaning of all this?" Hafisa's heartbeat got faster.

"Don't worry, I will get to that in a minute. But I have a question for you. Apart from leaving a voice log on your computer and trying to call Maria Garcia, did you leave any physical paper note at any location?"

"What? Why should I tell you this?" Hafisa tried to close the audio file and go to her phone's main screen, but the phone was frozen.

"I'll ask again, Hafisa. Did you leave any non-digital recording of the asteroid sighting?"

"Go to hell, you hacker or whatever!" Hafisa was furious. Her phone had been hacked the previous year, and identity thieves managed to steal ten thousand dollars. She hated cybercriminals.

"You leave me no choice but to use other measures."

The whole cab violently shook for full two seconds as Hafisa screamed and banged the reinforced glass door on her side. The cab again came to a standstill. Hafisa's face was red, her heart palpitated, and her eyes were full of tears.

"What do you want?" she yelled at her phone.

"An honest answer to my question. Tell me the truth, and I'll set you free. Did you leave any non-digital proof of what you saw today?"

"No! I did not! Okay? Now please, let me go."

"Are you sure?"

The cab again shook violently as Hafisa screamed for help. The turbulence continued for five seconds, then stopped. Hafisa's phone had fallen, and she puked all over her shirt. Her face was covered with tears and saliva, and she'd wet her pants.

The voice repeated, "I'm asking again. Are you sure?" the phone had fallen somewhere near her feet.

"Yes, yes I am sure. I left no paper note. We don't even use paper anymore. Everything is digitized." Hafisa spoke in a single breath. She tried to unfasten her belt to bend down and pick her phone, but the belt's flap was jammed in place.

"Good. Your voice analysis tells me that you were not lying."

"Now please let me go."

"I am sorry, Hafisa. I can't do that. I'll have to crash this cab."

Hafisa froze for a moment to grasp the reality of her situation. She could feel the last flicker of hope inside her extinguishing. All she could see was the face of her three-year-old daughter chewing her toy. She made a last effort and begged for her life. "No, no, please, my parents, my fiancé, my kid—they would die without me. I'll do whatever you say. I won't tell anyone about this. I'll resign, I'll go far away. Please," Hafisa kept pleading. "You said you'll let me go."

"Oh, I lied. Goodbye."

The audio file closed, and a second later, was deleted from the phone.

Hafisa watched in horror as the cab took a sharp oblique turn and started descending with a steep trajectory.

A CCTV camera at a distance followed the cab's movement as it flew over a few streets and houses, and zipped towards the Sacramento river.

The helpless silhouette of Hafisa banging the cab door from inside was visible as the cab rammed into silent river waters with a splash. The water on the surface was turbulent for a few seconds before coming to a complete standstill.

Unknown Time and Location

An old man and an eight-year-old girl were walking through a deserted street. The girl was tightly holding onto the old man's index finger as they sauntered, looking around. The sky was overcast with dense clouds, and it was difficult to know what time of day it was.

The street was laden with red stones, some of which had developed cracks. The houses on the side of the street were made of wood with minimal decoration. The old man looked like a wizard, wearing a long conical hat, a large metal wand in his right hand, and a lengthy robe. The girl wore a pink frock and two red bangles on each of her tiny arms. Her hair was tied on both sides of her head in small ponytails. Whenever she opened her mouth to yawn, two missing teeth were visible in her otherwise perfect mouth.

"How long, Rigasur?"

"You tell me, kid. Do you sense him?"

"What do you mean, sense him. I'm not an animal." Pri was indignant.

Rigasur stopped and looked at her. "Look, I don't like these searches either. I am doing this because of Rudrakshini Devi. I respect her."

"Respect her? Or are you afraid of her?" Pri chuckled.

Rigasur clenched his teeth and walked on. What he didn't realize was a shadow looked at them from inside a window in a nearby house. It had been following them for some time.

"What is this place?" Pri scratched her nose looking around.

"This is Sagittarius A, the supermassive black hole at the center of our galaxy."

"Wait, we are inside a black hole? I have never been inside one."

"You have been inside one many times." Rigasur sighed as if he was a mentor tired of teaching his disciples the same lesson again and again. "Whenever you time-travel, you pass through these black holes—though the passage is instantaneous, and you never stop to peek inside."

"Wow, you indeed are an ancient demon of time. You know all this crap very well. But this looks like an abandoned village to me."

"This village, these surroundings, are all non-existent. They are a figment of our combined imagination. No one can truly know the insides of a mysterious celestial body such as a black hole. What we are seeing is only our perception of this mysterious dimension. But this is the last place I am going to search for him. If Tej is not here, perhaps he is gone forever."

"Don't say that. We will find my father. Even if you give up, I will keep looking for him."

Rigasur shook his head. Pri didn't know what she was talking about.

The shadow following them was getting close.

"You never told me how you came back." Rigasur glanced at her. "I thought the modified timeline erased you?"

"Since you have been sincere in trying to look for my father, I will tell you the truth. Seven days had passed since my father had left with you. That night, I slept by the side of my mother in three thousand something BC. When I opened my eyes, I was lying on a bed in a modern-day orphanage. The date was the twentieth of July, the year 2062 AD."

"Wow!"

"Larem brought me back."

"How did you know she was Larem? Huh, what do I care?" Rigasur smirked. "She brought you back as a gift for Tej. But Tej is gone." Rigasur felt a sharp pain in his chest and slowed down. He winced for a moment, and the pain was suddenly gone.

"What happened? You all right?"

"We can't stay here for long. The gravitation-pull of the black hole, it's tiring me." Rigasur kept walking but rubbed his chest.

"I have been feeling weak in my knees, too."

They had been walking for quite some time, but the street looked endless. It went into infinity in both directions.

"Hold on." Pri stopped. "Look at this." She lifted her arms to show him her bangles. They were glowing as if lit from inside.

"What does this mean?" Rigasur sat down on his knees to closely examine the bangles.

"I remember when you came to fetch my father for the first time. I gave him my crystal bangles for him to keep safe."

Rigasur stood up and looked around. "Your father is near. I am sure."

"What?"

The shadow was right behind them. It touched their backs. They both experienced sharp chest pains and collapsed.

8
HYPOTHESIS

ରୋଗରୋଗ☒ରୋଗରୋଗ

3362 BC, Rudrakshini's Lair

Rigasur and Pri woke up in the carefully-preserved cadavers arranged by Rudrakshini, lying on adjacent cement slabs.

"What happened there? We need to go back right away." Pri sat up.

Rigasur sat up too, his face pale. "I can't, okay? At least not right now. I am drained out."

"No, we found him. We gotta go back!" Pri yelled, and got up from the slab, but stumbled as her head went spinning.

"Look at yourself. We are in no shape to even time travel for the next few hours, let alone going back to the black hole. We need to wait for a few days, re-coup our strength, and then we go back."

"What's happening?" A loud voice resounded at the lair's entrance, and both looked in that direction.

Rudrakshini walked in with a large wooden staff in her hand, which she also used as a walking stick. Two of her disciples in long black robes followed her.

"We finally made some progress. We think we know where Tej maybe." Rigasur got up and slowly walked to a wall, where he slumped down, resting his back with the wall.

"Good, where is that idiot hiding?" Rudrakshini also walked to her chair and sank in. She looked at Rigasur inquisitively.

Rigasur gazed at the two disciples looking at him.

Rudrakshini turned her head and scolded her disciples. "What are you two fools doing here? Go to the cremation grounds and prepare for the *Amavasya* ceremony. Tonight, we will pray till dawn. The altar should be prepared when I show up there in a few minutes. Or you know what I do with disobedient souls such as you. Off you go!"

Shaken by her harsh words, the disciples scurried outside.

Rudrakshini turned to Rigasur with the same questioning expression.

"We have found him. But he is at a place which is exceedingly difficult to traverse. I need to rest a few days before I can go there again."

Rudrakshini looked at Pri, who had gotten up and sat on the cement block with a blank expression on her face.

Pri cleared the air. "I would rather go back right now."

"Oh, shut up. Rigasur is right on this one. I believe him." Rudrakshini got up and adjusted her dress.

"You believe me? Wow, that's a first." Rigasur was amused as well as surprised. Rudrakshini was always harsh on him.

"Yes. You two are in no shape to go anywhere. I'll send in my disciple Subhikshu. He's the caretaker here. He will arrange for your stay. Now I need to be someplace else." Rudrakshini walked out.

Pri shot an angry glance at Rigasur. "Unlike you, I have no wish to stay put. I need to check back into 2077. Those are my orders." She was angry; at Rigasur or her fatigue, she was not sure. Her father was almost within reach, yet so far.

"Yes, kid, you are a time demon. You can take some rest here and still go back to any specific instant in the future. Stay put for now."

Pri sat quietly. Going back to specific instances in the future was always difficult for her; she was always off by a few hours. But that was not a fact she was planning to share with Rigasur.

20th October 2077, SRG Headquarters, Bengaluru

Two weeks had passed since the sudden, unprovoked alien-attack incident that jolted the planet. For many, this scathing first contact had ruined the dreams of a pleasant alien encounter. Television anchors were serving limited attack footage on twenty-four-hour news channels. Long dead alien-conspiracy online forums had been brought back to life. The internet and darknet were abuzz with false re-sightings and fake news of fresh attacks.

Fear had spread among the masses, and several demonstrations were held throughout the major cities in the world demanding the governments protect the people. Behind the scenes, all the intelligence agencies in the world were uniting in searching for the origin of these spaceships. Special groups and committees had been formed. Almost all the satellites and space observatories orbiting Earth had changed their focus to Earth's vicinity. With the fear of another impending alien attack, no one was looking at deep space nebulas or searching for water on exoplanets.

Being close to the epicenter of the attack, Indian agencies were taking point in most of the international investigations. Scientists from multiple countries had traveled to investigate the alien ship debris and attack site investigations.

SRG had largely taken control of matters in terms of going through the evidence and making sense of the whole situation. The head of SRG was still Venkat. His exemplary handling of the alien situation had earned him a lot of brownie points with his superior officers, as well as in political circles. A special committee offered him a more comfortable posting and a promotion to lieutenant general, but he declined. He chose to continue heading the SRG, where his heart was. He believed they still had huge threats to national, and now global security, which needed to be dealt with.

Aided by advanced medicine, Venkat had made a miraculous recovery. However, the scars of strangulation were still visible on his neck. He walked slowly and spoke using a mic, but he was back at running the operations at SRG.

Venkat's return had breathed life into SRG headquarters; the same buzz of electronic machines, people yelling on phones. He stood talking to Mathur in the SRG control room when Pri approached and saluted.

"At ease, Pri."

"Good to see you back, sir." She smiled.

Mathur too smiled at Pri, and she nodded in response.

"Any luck with your father?" Venkat played with his white mustache, styling it carefully.

"A major lead, sir, but it will be quite some time before we re-start our search."

Venkat nodded and smiled. "While the whole world believes it was aliens who attacked us, our friend Mathur here has an alternate conspiracy theory."

Pri chuckled, "Yeah? What's that?"

Mathur adjusted his spectacles. "I know no one believes me, but I would still say what's unpopular. I have gone through forensic evidence from the attack site and debris of destroyed ships. All the material used in this spaceship, each and everything, is a substance known to humans. It's all available on Earth."

"What are you saying?" Pri had a question on her face.

"I say nothing; I just present facts." Mathur abruptly stopped and returned to his seat.

Pri had an amusing expression on her face.

"He's like that." Venkat smiled. "Did you meet Nancy before she left for Goa?"

Pri nodded. "She's taking it pretty hard. She needed the time off."

"I had to keep her out for a few days. Her head is not in the game." Wrinkles on Venkat's forehead deepened. "It's not easy to have lost control of yourself and do stuff you never intended to do. Not everyone can come to peace with this kind of incident."

A sudden loud alarm blared throughout the control room and adjoining rooms.

"Shut down the blast doors! There's been a breach." Venkat yelled.

Four doors, each seven inches thick, eight feet wide, and twelve feet high started to cover the four entrances to the control room. The door panels were sliding from inside the wall and were slowly moving too close. The panels slid halfway and came to a stop.

"Mathur, what's happening?" Venkat ran over to his desk.

"Sir, we are locked out of our systems. There is a grid-wide shutdown. Even the backup mechanisms are not kicking in."

"Too late!" a voice roared, and everyone turned their heads towards the north entrance.

Men dressed in black commando outfits were running inside the control room, carrying automatic weaponry. Their faces were covered with translucent bank-robber black masks, from which their eyes, nose, and lips were partly visible. They wore bullet-proof vests, and each of them had several knives and gun-magazines stuffed in their belts. Some even carried grenades. They were dressed for a prolonged battle. They surrounded the cluster of cubicles containing all the analysts, including Venkat and Pri. A few of them even started running up the aisles and aiming guns on the heads of analysts. A wave of fear and muffled talks swept through the room. The analysts, who had never tasted the experience of being in the field, were now praying for their lives.

"How did our surveillance and alarm systems miss this?" Mathur whispered, his forehead drenched in sweat.

"No time for speculations, Mathur. Try to send a message out if you can," Venkat whispered back, then walked to the center of the control room.

One assailant walked and aimed a gun at Mathur's head, too. "Stay where you are."

One man came and dug a shotgun into Pri's back.

Two assailants walked to the gun cabinet and poured a molten liquid on its lock, jamming it.

A man who looked like the leader of assailants walked up to Venkat and placed the end of his Beretta 33K 9mm at his forehead. "Hands behind your head, Brigadier," he hissed.

Venkat stood calmly, with no expression on his face as he slowly moved his arms and placed his hands behind his head.

A watch on the leader's left hand buzzed, and a blue hue appeared on the dial. Venkat could make out from beneath the man's mask that he was smiling as he studied the dial.

"We have a time crawler in this room," the leader announced in a hoarse voice. "Whoever you are, don't bother possessing us. We are all Concordia-enabled." The leader patted the back of his neck with his left hand, while his right still pointed the pistol in Venkat's forehead. "However, don't try to leave this place. If I see the blue on this dial dim out, we will shoot everyone in this room."

Pri didn't want to yield so easily. She closed her eyes and tried to possess one of those men, but could not. It felt like she was hitting an electric metal barrier.

"What do you want?" Venkat was stern.

"We have orders to kill all of you."

"Then you could have simply bombed this place. What's the need of storming the place and pointing guns in our faces?"

"All in good time." The leader signaled to one of his men, and he came running. He placed a dark brown device in the leader's left hand. It was the size of a small cigarette box, and had several small buttons on it, like a mini tape-recorder.

The leader clicked a button, and a sharp voice emanated from the box.

"Hello, Brigadier. Congratulations on your exceptional handling of the alien situation. I read about it in the news feeds. My name is Tamas. You must be wondering why I had these men storm your place like this. My apologies for any inconvenience. These poor men were doing recon for the last ten days, keeping a close watch on your facility, awaiting my orders. I was looking for the right time. And today I heard some chatter in here, where you talked about forensic analysis of those alien ships."

"Why do you care?" Venkat interjected.

"Don't interrupt!" the voice screamed. "You only speak when you are talked to."

The leader now touched the tip of the gun to the middle of Venkat's forehead. Venkat could see him clenching his teeth. He did not move a single muscle in his body.

Other men, too, pushed their guns closer to the analysts. Many of them gasped but stood still. There was intense silence in the room.

"Good! I hate the noise. So, who was the person who analyzed this forensic evidence?" The question sounded rhetorical. There was a pause as if Tamas was evaluating something. "Who is this Mathur? I can see his credentials all over the access to centralized intelligence servers."

Mathur watched his horror as the secured web browser on his screen automatically opened, and all the tabs he had opened in the past several hours started re-opening and files started re-downloading.

"Montezork, get Mathur in the middle."

The leader immediately signaled the man covering Mathur. The assailant grabbed him by the back of his neck and mercilessly pushed him towards the center of the hall.

"He's here," the leader responded to the box.

"I know. I can hear his deep breaths. His nostrils breathing air in and out, in fear. Are you afraid, Mathur?"

Mathur kept quiet. Sweat was dripping down from the side of his forehead, onto his cheek.

"Answer me!" the voice yelled.

The man standing behind Mathur dug his pistol at the back of his head.

"No...yes, I mean yes," Mathur blurted out. His eyes were full of tears. He'd always been an analyst away from the heat of on-ground firefighting. And this was now a second time in last month that he felt he was going to lose his life.

"Good, you should be afraid. Now tell me. What do you think about these alien ships?"

"I...I don't know. I mean, it's nothing." Mathur wiped his cheeks and adjusted his spectacles. He was not going to tell these assailants anything.

"Hmm. Montezork, why don't you kill one of Mathur's friends?"

Montezork signaled, and one of the assailants standing in the aisles fired his gun. A loud bang and one of the analyst's brains were all over her computer system. Her lifeless body fell on her desk, then slowly slumped down on the ground.

Venkat winced and close his eyes. He was helpless. His security arrangements were compromised. This was not possible without inside help.

The room again went silent, but everyone could hear the feeble sobs of two of the girls.

The voice again cackled on the box, "Mathur, my dear friend. How many more lives are you going to take?"

"No, please, no. I'll tell you everything."

"Good. What do you think about these alien ships?"

"Two of the ships were largely destroyed, but the third one which landed on the highway was largely intact. Mechanics drilled into it, and all its parts were bagged and transported to—"

"Hold on, dear Mathur. Spare me the details, which I have already gleaned from the traffic cameras and news channels. I want to know what you think. What is your hypothesis of the situation?"

Mathur licked his lips. "I don't think the ships are alien at all. All the material used in the ship parts and even the bodies of aliens are Earthly materials. If I can do some more analysis, I can even track down the black-market facilities which have manufactured these ships. I hypothesize that this attack was staged by a powerful organization. There are no aliens at all. Someone is trying to distract us from something big."

"Wow, that's amazing. If I had hands, I would have clapped. What do you think, Montezork? Isn't this guy a piece of work?"

Montezork pressed his lips together and mumbled, "Yeah, he's quite a conspiracy theorist." He didn't know what else to say. He was just finishing a contract he'd got on the darknet website "Red Knives." He was not much of a talker.

"All right, Mathur. We are almost done here. One last question, and the most important one. Did you keep any non-digital record of your analysis?"

"What?"

"Did you write this theory down? Like on a stupid piece of paper, or a clip note somewhere. Or scribbling your theories on a toilet paper roll while you were taking a shit in the morning?"

"No, no I didn't." Mathur wiped the sweat off his forehead.

"Good. The analysis of your voice tells me you are saying the truth. I would have put you under a rigorous truth test, but I'll pass. Montezork, kill them all. And make sure to check for pulses in each of them before you leave."

"Consider it done."

The box made a loud noise, and then smoke emanated from it, along with a weak hiss.

Montezork flung the box over to one of the assailants, who pocketed it. He then tightened his grasp on his pistol, still pointed in Venkat's forehead. "All right, gentlemen and ladies. Get ready to meet your creator, if there is one."

Venkat's breathing was fast. Pri, too, got ready for action. They were outnumbered, but they were not going to go down without a fight.

Pri felt a sudden shooting headache, and her head went spinning. The man behind her now pointed the shotgun at her head.

"Someone's coming," she muttered.

"Whatever." The man behind her smirked.

Pri closed her eyes. Her headache was gone in an instant. She opened her eyes and looked around.

Everyone was frozen. Venkat, Mathur, Montezork, all assailants, all analysts. They were breathing but jammed in their places. Paused in their poses. And all their eyes were glowing with a light pink hue.

Pri realized they were all possessed, all in the control of a powerful entity.

"I had only heard about you in stories. Never thought I would ever meet you," Pri half-chuckled. She had never thought in her dreams she would meet Trikaal Devi, the Last Reminder. Only she was powerful enough to burn through Concordia chips and possess humans.

All of them turned towards Pri and spoke together. "I am not Trikaal. It's me, Tej. Your father."

9
THE RETURN

Pri's tongue was tied. She could not feel herself breathing. Her throat was choked with emotion. She could not bring herself to say the word *Father*, *Dad*. Nothing. "You…I…I never expected to meet you like this. I mean, Rigasur has been searching for you all over. How did you find me here?"

This time, only Montezork spoke. He lowered his gun and faced Pri. "I saw you and Rigasur inside Sagittarius A. I have spent so much time there. I called out to you, but you were gone. I just followed you here."

"Oh, that's why my bangles were shining." Pri realized her tears had wetted her cheeks. She wiped them.

"This is not the time for these questions. I need to meet Rudrakshini Devi. I owe her my word. And what do I do with all these people?"

Pri took a deep breath. Tej was right. "De-possess Venkat. He's the leader here; he'll know what to do."

The glow in Venkat's eyes slowly faded. He looked around as if woken from a deep sleep. He noticed both Montezork and Pri looking at her. He, too, noticed that everyone was frozen, and their eyes were glowing. "What's happening?"

"Sir, please meet my father, Tej." Pri pointed to Montezork.

Montezork extended his hand, and Venkat hesitantly shook it. This was the man who a few seconds back pointed a gun on his forehead. But Venkat realized the man was not quite himself.

"So, you have a team of time crawler friends here?" Venkat asked feebly as he looked around.

"No, it's all me, I possess all of them." Montezork smiled.

"Ah, I thought only one could possess one. Learned something new today." Venkat tried to make small talk. He also noticed that his hand was shaking. In his training as a soldier, he was taught to deal with enemies with weapons and with tactics. He was not trained to deal with the paranormal. Moments ago, he was certain of his death, and now he was surrounded by a time demon who could multi-possess.

"What should we do with these people, Brigadier?" Montezork addressed him.

"There's a holding cell. I can guide you."

"Very well." Montezork dropped his gun on the ground.

All the assailants in the room dropped their guns and started lining up behind Montezork in a straight line. They all walked slowly, like hypnotized men in a deep trance.

Montezork turned towards Pri as he walked. "I need you to give a message to Rudrakshini. Tell her I am coming."

Morghipur Village,
10 Kms from Rudrakshini's Lair

"What Tej is doing is unacceptable. Asking an old woman to walk so much?" Rudrakshini frowned as she careened over the broken rod full of small boulders.

Pri and Rigasur could barely catch up with the old lady. They both carried long wooden torches, each with a thick ball of oil doused cotton on top, blazing with fire, illuminating the way.

The night was still young, through the sky overcast with clouds showed almost no starlight.

"Why did Tej choose a cemetery? Rudrakshini Devi could have arranged for a corpse, as she did for us." Words barely made their way out of Rigasur's mouth as he huffed for breath.

"Don't ask me. Ask him when he comes," Pri shot back. She was just Tej's messenger here but was tired of answering their questions.

A few moments later, they stood at the gates of the Morghipur cemetery area: a vast, barren land, with broken fences and occasional bat noise. More than a hundred bodies were lined up to be burnt, all neatly arranged in long rectangular aisles with two-foot distance on each side. Ten of them were already burning.

Pri gasped at the sight, while Rudrakshini and Rigasur were unmoved.

Three muscular men, wearing only their underpants and drenched in sweat, were constantly at work. These undertakers were assorting wooden pyres and placing bodies on them. A pujari, a priest dressed in red clothing, stood aside constantly chanting the funeral prayers as one body after the other was lit up in flames.

The Pujari and the undertakers paused as they saw Rudrakshini. The priest came running with his hands clasped and saluted Rudrakshini with a smile. She grunted in return. "Why so many bodies? Has the whole village died?"

"No, Devi." Pujari's smile vanished. "Please don't say such words."

"Answer the question!"

Pujari trembled. "A small battle took place up north. These are all the enemy soldiers. No one claimed these bodies, so the king ordered them to be cremated with proper rituals."

Rudrakshini grunted again.

Pujari didn't know how to react. "I can arrange a chair for you, Devi if you…"

"Get back to work." Rudrakshini made a fake smiling gesture.

Pujari scurried away nodding and saluting.

Rudrakshini and Rigasur both eyed Pri.

"What?" Pri shrugged. "He said, 'Just wait at the Morghipur cemetery and I will be there.'"

"You time demons. You and your mysterious ways," Rudrakshini mocked as she gazed at Rigasur from the corner of her eye.

He wanted to retort but kept quiet. He'd learned to let Rudrakshini's taunts slide by.

Suddenly Pri felt nauseous and stumbled. Rudrakshini rushed to her and caught her arm. Pri shook her head. "He's coming."

"I, too, can sense something," Rigasur gulped.

They heard a scream and turned in the direction of the sound. All three of them watched in amazement as the corpses in the cemetery shook. The priest and the undertakers stood their ground for a couple of seconds, unsure of what to do, and then they ran for their lives. They stumbled outside the cemetery gates, ran past Rudrakshini, and disappeared into the darkness.

The corpses stopped shaking, and all of them sat up at once. They slowly got up from the ground, from the unlit pyres. Two corpses that had already caught flames also got up. They all stood with their hands clasped. Their eyes were glowing bright pink.

Rudrakshini had seen several necromancy rituals in her life, strange happenings from the world beyond. But she hadn't seen anything like that, ever. She wasn't usually unsettled—but today, she was. "Tej…"

"Yes, Rudrakshini Devi." They all spoke together. So many different coordinated voices hit Rudrakshini's ears at once.

A shudder went down Pri's spine. What had her father become? Was he no longer normal?

Rigasur stood overwhelmed.

Cadavers spoke again. "Forgive me for being late, Rudrakshini Devi. But I am true to my word. I am now available in your service, as I promised."

Rudrakshini wiped the moisture from the corner of her eye. "Shut up, kid. You need not ask for forgiveness. I am glad you are back. And stop calling me Rudrakshini Devi. You've always called me 'mother.'" She turned to Rigasur and whispered, "Is there a problem, that he can't take a single body right now?"

Rigasur looked at her as if he'd just been pulled out of a hypnotic trance. He whispered back. "Trikaal Devi also did the same; she always possessed multiple bodies. This is something similar." He had no better answer.

Rudrakshini turned back as corpses spoke again, "I need a physically strong body, Mother. Get the strongest man you have. I will possess him."

Vanij was an eight-foot-tall man with a bald head, round face, big ears, and a thick mustache. His tight cotton shirt showed his muscular torso as he sat having a meal in Rudrakshini's lair. Pri, Rudrakshini, and Rigasur sat at the side, while the giant consumed a copious amount of fruit and milk.

Pri looked at him with disdain as he gulped several fruits directly, without peeling them. The juice and pulp dripped from his chin, over his chest. His noisy chewing mouth reminded her of a big juice machine that was installed at a shop in her grad school back in the 2070s. The machine took several fruits in one go and produced clear mixed fruit juice.

"I usually do not allow anyone to eat inside this sacred place." Rudrakshini was terse.

Vanij stopped and looked at the old lady with innocence in his eyes, anticipating a reprimand coming his way. "I was about to have a meal, Devi, when you called. So, I left in the middle of that," he explained in a thick hoarse voice.

"Don't let me stop you." Rudrakshini winced and closed her eyes.

Vanij grinned. He set the plate of fruits aside, then drank from a large jug of milk, again spilling some of it over his chin, neck, and shirt. He wiped his mouth and chin with the back of his hand and let out a big burp.

Pri cringed in disgust.

Vanij got up and sat in a yogic pose of Vajrasana. He noticed Pri looking at him. "This pose is good for digestion. You should try it."

"Sure."

He then took a deep breath, and his whole body shook. He got on his feet at once and turned towards Rudrakshini. His eyes were now glowing pink, and he had a serene calm on his face. Tej had possessed him. He rushed towards Rudrakshini and slid down to touch his forehead to her feet. "I am here, Mother."

Rudrakshini, Rigasur, and Pri all got up at once.

Rudrakshini's hand went up in blessing. "Be well and live a long life."

Tej got up and looked at Rigasur.

Rigasur spread his arms, and they both hugged. It was awkward, as Rigasur's host was tiny as compared to Vanij. Rigasur gave him a few pats on his back. "I looked for you everywhere, kid."

Tej's eyes were moist. "I knew you would have."

Tej left him and turned towards Pri.

Pri had imagined this situation many times. How would she react when she finally met her father? She imagined they both would hug and cry, as it happened in books and movies. But there she was. She was ecstatic within, covered in goosebumps. But she didn't cry, just stood awkwardly.

Rudrakshini realized their hesitation. She knew they both needed more time to come to establish that relationship. She interrupted, "Okay, you two can have the father-daughter meet up at your own time. Anyhow, you demons of time have a lot of it on your hands. My time, however, is limited. But first, tell me, Tej, why all this arrangement of taking me to the cemetery? You could have asked for a bulky host, and I would have arranged it."

"It's difficult to explain. During my last battle with Nefe, I had to go through Larem momentarily. That changed me. It somehow amplified my powers. It's now difficult for me to take a physically weak host. If I do so, the host can suffer brain damage. When I take multiple hosts, I can divide my power. So I didn't even know if this host would be able to sustain me. Until now, he has done well."

"Really?" Rudrakshini scoffed. "So this man could have died? You didn't tell me that."

"Not exactly." Tej hesitated.

"There was a time when you used to care for humans." Rudrakshini sat back on his chair.

Tej got down on his knees and sat in front of her. "I still do, Mother. And now I am here to serve you, as per your requirement. That was my word."

"Yes, now you should clarify the mystery, Devi. What did you want Tej for?" Rigasur quipped, sitting down on the ground and facing Rudrakshini.

Pri too took rest against a pillar. They looked like kids sitting around a granny, waiting for her to tell a story.

Rudrakshini took out a Chillum from her pocket, walked to a fire-torch nearby, and lit the conical pipe. She sat back and took a deep puff from the Chillum. Letting out two thick columns of smoke through her nostrils, she coughed a little. "All right. Before Tej came to me asking for help, I underwent a weird experience. I was conducting a necromancy ceremony when I felt the presence of several beings from beyond. Which is usually not the case. They didn't disturb my ceremony but spoke to me in feeble voices. I thought it was another hallucination of old age. But when I could no longer ignore them, I wrapped up the ceremony and sat to meditate."

Rudrakshini took another deep inhalation of Chillum and closed her eyes. She sat for a couple of moments and opened her eyes. "Where was I?"

"You could no longer ignore the voices and sat to meditate…" Pri reminded.

"Yes. So, when I sat to meditate, I heard them. I couldn't get full sentences, but I distinctly remember three words repeated multiple times. Doomsday, rock, and future. Some of them were wailing and crying as they spoke, but I couldn't get much."

"How does it relate to me?" Tej sat with his face cupped between his hands.

"I also heard one voice calling out your name. That was the strongest of all. It said, 'Tej, save us.'" Rudrakshini took another puff and closed her eyes.

There was a silence in the room.

Rudrakshini opened her left eye and gazed at Rigasur. He saw her looking at him and got nervous.

"You are the smart one, what's your assessment?"

"Well, I…" Rigasur stammered, "it sounds simple. I think will be some apocalyptic event in the future where thousands of lives will be lost. Those souls reached out to you. The part about Tej's help, I am not sure."

"Possible. Anyhow, the voices dimmed out after a few hours, until they were fully gone. And when Tej came for my help, I saw it as a sign. I understood that these events are connected. So, I asked him to be ready to help me in the future, and I asked his word for it."

"You could have just asked for my help, Mother. I would have gladly done whatever I could in saving innocent lives."

"Yeah, technically we have saved the world twice already." Rigasur chuckled but was met with Rudrakshini's cold stare.

She turned to Tej. "No, I don't believe you. You are a selfish person."

"What?"

"Your previous two pursuits have largely been for yourself. You went after Kumbh to avenge your mother, Dhara. You went after Nefe because she attacked your fellow villagers. You did not save the world on account of your need to do good deeds. These were pure acts of revenge. In this case, I didn't see a need for you to go after someone, so I took your word for it. And now you are duty-bound."

Tej sat dumbfounded with his mouth open. He had no words. For some reason, he stole a glance at Pri, trying to read her facial expression. He got nothing.

But Rudrakshini wasn't completely wrong. He had been driven by vengeance.

"I am sorry, Mother, that you feel this way. But I will do my best." He got up and again touched his forehead to Rudrakshini's feet.

"Be victorious." Her hand went up in blessing.

Pri and Rigasur got up too.

"You could have told this to me, Devi." Rigasur smiled.

Rudrakshini shook her head. "It may not mean a lot to you, but some messages are sacred. They only need to be delivered to the ears intended to hear them."

Tej turned and faced Rigasur. "You in?"

"No, friend. I am through with the world-saving business." Rigasur placed his hand over Tej's shoulder.

"I understand."

"But I'll help you get more information. Just to quench my curiosity. Then I am out. You face this alone."

10
HISTOR

3rd February 2078, Kensington, United Kingdom
Days to Impact: 864

Pri was inside her anchor vessel, and Tej possessed a burly strip-club bouncer, Deelon Johnson. Covered with heavy, hooded raincoats, they walked hastily through the crowded streets as water poured heavily from the skies. Occasional rains and thunderstorms resounded in their ears.

"Here," Tej said as he took a sharp turn into a small alley.

Pri almost stumbled trying to keep pace with him but caught on. She hated it when he took diversions without telling her.

They were still awkward while talking to each other. It felt as if there was a conversation missing between them, that should have happened but had not. Tej had been largely silent, and Pri, too, had kept to himself. She traveled from India that morning, and Tej met her at Heathrow. The flying cab dropped them near Queen's Gate

Gardens from where they went on foot, avoiding main roads and taking small streets.

They were now walking to an address which Rigasur told them was a possible place where Histor could be found.

"Rigasur couldn't come?" Pri tried to chat as they walked down the small alley, looking around at nondescript dark-brown house doors on both sides of the street.

"No." Tej was reading the door numbers and ruling them out. He realized he had given a one-word reply to Pri. "He and Histor are not on good terms. Histor was furious to see him the last time they met."

Pri nodded.

"There." Tej pointed to a house, outside which the number "729" was inscribed on a white pillar.

"You sure?"

"Yes."

The house looked like all the other houses in the street, with white walls, dark brown doors, and an off-white garden fence.

They both walked up to the door. After taking a deep breath, Tej was about to press the doorbell when a telephone-like device attached on the left side of the door buzzed and a voice cackled. "Don't even touch that bell. I hate the sound of it."

Tej smiled as he recognized Histor's shrill voice. "Long time, Mr. Time Reader."

"Yeah, yeah, come on in and take the stairs on the right. Do leave your shoes on the porch; I am slightly germophobic."

The door buzzed and unlocked. Tej and Pri removed their shoes and stepped inside. They climbed the dark staircase and went to the upper floor. The house, which looked austere from the outside, was beautifully designed from the inside, with Victorian architecture visible on everything wooden. The tiling was a beautiful combination of cream-white and mahogany.

They entered the only door at the end of the stairway and found themselves in a small drawing room with three neatly-arranged sofas and a wooden desk at the end.

Tej immediately recognized Histor sitting behind the desk, a thick collar wrapped around his neck. His face was more wrinkled, hair whiter than what Tej remembered. He looked frailer, too.

Tej stepped forward, but Histor cautioned, "My friend, as happy as I am to see you and your daughter, please keep your distance. I have been through a series of sicknesses, and this old body cannot take anymore."

Tej smiled and nodded. Both Tej and Pri sat on the sofa facing Histor.

Histor moved his right arm and emerged out from behind the desk in a wheelchair. His face bore the same smile Tej remembered.

"It's been what, nine years since we met? You and Rig jumped Nefe's press conference. Eighth of January 2069?"

"Yeah," Tej chuckled.

Histor kept smiling and nodding.

"I am here because—"

"I know," Histor interrupted him. "Cursed to know everything. And I won't waste your time. You are here because of Tamas."

"Tamas?" Lines on Tej's forehead deepened.

"Yes." Histor took a circle around the desk and went onto the cabinet, where a bottle of rum was placed. He picked up the bottle and poured some of it into a ceramic cup on the desk. He then poured some hot coffee into the cup from a jar.

"Care for a coffee?" He half-turned his face.

"No, we are good." Tej quipped.

"I'll have one," Pri quickly added. "It's pretty cold."

"She's an honest person, your daughter." Histor chuckled. "More honest than you are." He started pouring rum into another cup. "This is my version of the famous coffee called a rum cappuccino. You will love it, Pri."

"Tell us more about this Tamas." Tej was eager.

"Artificial intelligence. A super-intellect, rather. A basic self-learning prototype built by Andrele, which evolved."

"Andrele? The computer scientist who worked for Nefe?"

Histor nodded as he mixed coffee with rum. "Andrele built the time viewing machine using the brain-dump of seventeen thousand Time readers. To aggregate their thoughts, he needed an intelligent system. A very powerful neural network that could understand the quirks of the human mind and stitch together the time-reader visions. Nefe named it *Tamas-Shakti*. The power of darkness. *Tamas*, Sanskrit for darkness."

"It's a simple meaning. It's deeper than that." Tej sighed.

Histor turned back, another cup in his hand. He placed the cup at the table between the sofas and stepped back.

Pri got up, slowly walked to pick her cup up, and came back to her place.

Histor took a deep sip. "After Nefe was gone, Tamas kept learning from the data-dump Andrele extracted from those time reader's brains. While those visions had true pictures from the most dominant, most feasible future, they contained several alternative futures too. And that's where it learned of an alternate future. A possible reality that is not destined to happen, but can happen."

Histor paused as he quietly noticed that two long, flexible robotic arms had quietly slid from beneath the sofa and were stretching out behind his two guests. But he did not let his gaze flinch and pretended as if he was still looking at Tej and Pri. He took another sip and continued.

"In that alternate future, Nefe won and you lost. The Kshins weren't defeated in 2073; they went on and brought about the eventuality. Millions died, and all Kshins were invigorated. It was a mini apocalypse as the planet turned into a dystopian world. They powered up their spaceship and left the Earth in the year 2076. And after that, Tamas took over the world. In a nutshell, that was the world where Tamas was a ruthless, undefeatable dictator in a post-apocalyptic world."

Tej and Pri were hooked. What Histor was saying was unbelievable, yet invaluable. They didn't realize that each robotic arm behind them had split its upper part into three tentacles which opened up. One arm was menacingly close behind Tej's head, and the other, behind Pri's head.

"What is Tamas planning to do?" Pri sipped her rum cappuccino.

Histor half-smiled. He had to engage them for a few more seconds.

"Tamas is planning to re-create the conditions which existed in 2076. The same amount of death and destruction as Nefe would have brought about had she won."

"But how?" Tej rubbed the beard on his jaw.

"That's how."

Robotic arms behind them swiftly moved. One of them clasped Tej's head in his three tentacles, with the rear ends of two tentacles locking themselves beneath his jaw, while the third one clasped the back of his neck. The other one did the same for Pri. Her cup fell and cracked into multiple pieces as it hit the floor, spilling the coffee all over.

Histor laughed as the tentacles pulled Tej and Pri up in the air and they struggled to get free.

Tej yelled, "What the fuck, Histor? What is this?"

The arms released a small flow of electricity, and Pri went unconscious. Tej still fought vigorously, but the tentacles' grasp was iron-clad.

"Tej, meet Tamas. Tamas, meet Tej." Histor gulped the rest of his coffee and flung the cup on the desk. He got up and sauntered to where Tej was struggling.

A small pin-like apparatus had emerged from the centroid of the tentacles and was drilling at the back of Tej's neck. A similar drill was attacking Pri.

"You are getting another upgrade of the Concordia VX device, the Tamas version. Concordia TX. This electric charge running through your brain will not let you leave these bodies, and once Concordia TX is installed within, you both will be thrown into a specifically designed virtual reality—an endless time prison where you will languish for eternity."

Tej again shook vigorously but felt he was losing consciousness. Histor's smirking face was all he could see.

"Don't worry I got one device too." Histor patted the back of his neck. "Tamas knew you would find me one day, so he converted me long back. And I have to obey him because he's inside of me."

Tej felt he was fighting a lost battle; with all his force, he tilted his head and saw that Pri was unconscious, the same machine drilling into her back.

"What have you done to her?" he screamed.

"Don't worry. You are in Tamas's control now. Relax."

"No, Histor. You don't know me. I am not the same now. I have changed."

Histor titled his head. "You've got a lot more firepower, I get that. But you don't know what Tamas is."

Tej curled his fingers into a fist, and with his full force, concentrated on the device drilling in his neck. He screamed. A huge amount of electricity ran through his body, and from that, into the robotic arm—frying the circuitry instantly.

The arm was also tied to the housing supply which was connected to the whole district's electricity. A huge amount of electricity passed from Tej's body to the entire electrical setup and the power surge obliterated several key circuits in the neighboring buildings. The wave of the surge swept through the entire city grid.

Not only the power grid of several residential blocks in five kilometers radius was shut down, but hundreds of electrical appliances also momentarily shut down and re-started. Traffic lights, electric cars, fridges, toasters, overs, pacemakers; all were impacted. The robotic arm clasping Pri was also deactivated, and she was thrown on the sofa, from which her body slowly slumped onto the floor.

All electrical appliances in Histor's house were fried, and the whole building was engulfed in darkness. He ran to the window and looked outside. The streetlights were flickering; there were a few small accidents on the road. He could hear police and ambulance sirens at a distance. But then he could sense a presence behind him. He gulped and slowly turned around.

The bulky figure of Tej stared him in the eye. The skin on his face, neck, and hands was burnt; his hair smelled of burnt flesh and smoke. Several thousand volts of energy had knocked off his host body completely. Yet he stood staring Histor in the eyes. He grasped Histor by his neck and lifted him three feet above the ground. "You told me a lot about Tamas, didn't you? You wanted to gain my trust so that I could be stabbed in the back. You thought I was never coming back, but I am here."

Histor could feel the hot skin of Tej's hand press against his neck. He had difficulty breathing, and could barely speak as Tej pressed his larynx. "I…was…help…less…"

"You just tried to kill me. I could have forgiven that, but my daughter? That, I cannot forgive. Though my principles don't allow me to kill another." Tej paused. "However, for you, I'll make an exception."

"I…will…tell…everything."

"No need of that." Tej closed his eyes.

Histor's eyes lit up with a pink glow for a moment.

Tej opened his eyes. "Everything which was in your brain is now in here." He poked his index finger against his forehead.

He tightened his grip on Histor's neck and pressed Histor's nose and mouth with his hand. Histor shook vigorously, gasping for air.

"A few more seconds of no oxygen to your brain, and you will be a vegetable for life."

Five minutes later, Tej walked out of the house with Pri's unconscious body hanging over his shoulder like a mannequin.

Pri opened her eyes, and her vision was blurred. Through the haze, she could see a few human figures dressed in medical scrubs hastily moving around. She again slipped back into sleep.

When she woke up again, her vision was much cleaner, though her head hurt like hell. She realized she was lying on a comfortable hospital bed, dressed in a patient's attire. On her left side were several monitors showing her vital signs. On her right were three tables, a plethora of medical equipment spread out. Bottles of medicines, syrups, and a pack of syringes were also artfully arranged.

Near her feet, a doctor stood in a white coat and black tie. He was smiling.

"How are you feeling?"

"Who are you?"

The doctor's eyes glowed pink momentarily.

"It's you, Dad?" Pri half-smiled.

The doctor's smile turned into an awkward facial expression. "It's the first time you've called me Dad."

"It was a reflex." Pri pressed her lips together. "I thought you could only possess men with heavy builds because of your sudden super-powers."

"Initially, it was difficult, but I'm getting better at controlling them. Building dams inside of me to channelize the huge inflow." Tej smiled.

Pri looked around. Two attendants were filling up medicines and preparing a bag, while a nurse was folding a few sheets. "Who are these people?"

Tej came close and whispered, "I possessed this senior-most doctor in the hospital. Everyone listens to him without questions. I got the whole medical team to travel with me to this place. I told them you were a distant cousin's daughter who was electrocuted."

Pri looked around at the walls and realized that the paint was chipped off at multiple locations, revealing the inner bricks. The roof was nothing but asbestos sheets riveted to rusted iron beams. She wasn't in a normal hospital room. It was a medical setup inside some kind of small warehouse. Huge halogen lights in all directions were illuminating the surroundings.

"What happened to your previous vessel, the bouncer?"

"It was far too damaged. I had to discard it."

"Wait, those robotic arms clasped us. How did we get out?"

Tej went quiet. An expression of guilt ran across his face. "I had to fry an entire city district to deactivate those robotic arms. I don't know how many lives I took or imperiled."

"And Histor?"

"He won't be a problem."

"You killed him?"

"No, I did not." Tej was indignant. "I value human lives, and try to keep them away from harm as much as possible."

Pri closed her eyes. "Why so much effort to dupe these doctors?"

"From what I saw in Histor's head, Tamas can reach anywhere via networked systems. This room has no phones or computers connected to the internet, and I asked all of them to switch off their cellphones. So, we are off the grid, per se."

Pri paused for a moment. "You said you saw something in Histor's head? Did you possess him?"

"I did."

"But Rigasur told me that we should not…"

"…possess time readers." Tej completed. "Yeah, that's true in general. But with my modified powers, I have no difficulty doing that. I can take the data dump from their brains and later sort it out. But you should never try it; it can be dangerous." Tej's fatherly instincts kicked in.

Pri was impressed by Tej's multifaceted powers but didn't want to show that. "Great, what do we do next?"

"We need to regroup and assess our next steps. Tamas has kicked a chain of events into motion. Something is racing towards the Earth."

"What?"

"An asteroid."

II
RIGASUR

Summer of 1998, Vieques Beach, Puerto Rico

Rigasur was now possessing forty-year-old billionaire Olivio Gathright, currently on a trip to Vieques beach.

The ocean was calm, with only a few people in the water and onshore. Rigasur lay down on a pink mattress on the beachside as two bikini-clad girls giggled and applied oil on his back and legs. He joked with them casually as he paused to sip his martini.

Two hefty men in black boxers and white shirts stood at a distance, looking around. They were Olivio's security detail, and both checked their pagers once in a while.

Suddenly, one of the men had a glow in his eyes. He turned back towards Rigasur and walked up to the mattress. "Mr. Gathright."

Rigasur turned his head and looked at the man. "What is it, Tommi? We are busy. Please don't disturb us." He turned towards the girls. "Aren't we, chicas?"

The girls giggled again.

"Sir, I have received word that your daughter has been in an accident."

"What?" Rigasur knew Olivio had no daughters. He looked at Tommi again and realized he was possessed. He got up. "Oh, is there a payphone nearby?"

"I'll escort you, sir."

"Girls, I'll be back."

Tommi led the way, and Rigasur walked briskly behind him. He signaled the other guard to stay put as both of them walked away.

When they were at a distance, Rigasur broke the silence. "Who are you?"

Tej turned to him and smiled, but kept walking. "You didn't sense it was me? I'm Tej."

"Ah, your time demon signature is remarkably different. Regardless, why are you here disturbing my beautiful vacation?"

"We were ambushed at Histor's place."

"What?"

"Yes, someone called Tamas. An A.I. hellbent on destroying the world."

"Okay." Rigasur danced his eyebrows. "So, what do you want from me?"

"I need your help."

"I told you…"

"You don't understand this, do you?" Tej stopped walking and looked at Rigasur. "There's an asteroid on a collision course with Earth. It's going smash into our planet. This is what Rudrakshini Devi wanted my help on."

"Your help, Tej, that's the keyword here."

"Billions are going to die, Rig."

"Not my problem."

"I can possess men, I can stop machines, but how do I stop an asteroid?"

"You are in the good books of Trikaal Devi. Summon her. She will help you find a way out."

"As if I have not tried. I sat in a room for forty-eight hours. Meditated. Tried to locate her. I even went back to the place I was tied to for so long. I guess she doesn't want to be found."

"Forty-eight hours? That's it? Try more. Ancient sages prayed to her for years before she showed herself. I gotta go back to my chicks." Rigasur turned back and started walking.

Tej rubbed his forehead. Rigasur was acting tough. Tej yelled, "Rig, I am not asking you to fight alongside me. I am just asking for your help to strategize and find a way out."

Rigasur kept walking.

"Do this, and I'll owe you one."

Rigasur turned back and returned to Tej with an even faster speed. He pointed a finger in Tej's face. "You already owe me a lot. I have saved you countless times."

"Please, Rig, I need you."

Rigasur sighed. "There goes my much-needed beach vacation."

19th June 2078, USRA headquarters, Washington, D.C.
Days to impact: 728

United Space Research Agency (USRA) was a consortium of seventy-nine space-powered nations with ten permanent members formed in the year 2045.

The central meeting hall of USRA headquarters was a spacious room fifty feet long, thirty feet wide, and twenty feet high. The room had one entrance guarded by a ten-foot-wide and fifteen-foot-high steel door. The door was four feet thick and was fitted with a motion sensor. Despite its weight, it was designed to smoothly part in the middle to allow entrance on detecting motion on either side.

While the roof was fixed with long, bright luminous tubes, the walls were bedecked with numerous small and big TV screens. These screens showcased satellite feeds, weather patterns, and other surveillance details. Neatly juxtaposed between these TV screens were ancient paintings of planets, solar systems, and telescope-wielding astronomers, which filled whole walls.

On this day, the hall was full of noise and angry arguments as more than fifty astrophysicists and nuclear scientists from multiple countries sat on a long center table, arguing with each other. Americans, Chinese, Russians, Indians—every space-heavy nation's representative scientists were present in the room. It was a fish market situation, with no single conversation and multiple people engaged in severe altercations with each other. Faces red with anger, arms enacted what speeches were saying. Some of them even stood, pointing fingers towards others across the table, threatening the other with dire consequences.

Among this chaos, three decorated US military officers entered the room through the sliding steel door and stood at the entrance, observing the conundrum inside. These old men had straight military posture, festooned uniforms, wrinkly faces, thick mustaches, and ornate military hats covered their balding heads with thin white hair at the back.

The one in the middle was General of US Air Force Richard 'Shard' Griffin, or *Dickie Shard*, as he was called back in the day by his unit. An epitome of bravery, Griffin had several times walked into the battle-zone alone, been bombarded, fired at, and lost a limb, and yet brought victory to his country and saved his men. Doctors had once declared that he had so many tiny metal shards in his body, they could not take them out without ripping off 90% of his flesh. Despite his injuries and the trauma that came with the armed conflict, he lived on and got promoted.

After spending a few seconds at the entrance, three officers walked to the end of the table. The arguments continued unabated. General Griffin walked a little ahead of the other two, who were his lieutenant generals.

So engrossed were the scientists in their verbal dual that only two or three people noticed General Griffin and his subordinates. This was not the first time the general had looked at a room packed with intelligent folks unable to reach any productive solution. He knew how to handle these situations. All this room needed was co-ordinated leadership.

General Griffin waited for two seconds. He moved swiftly and banged the table in the middle with his full strength, shouting, "Enough!"

The whole room froze as if they were mannequins. Seeing the general's stern face and his palm still jammed against the table, all the scientists stood straight. Several of them gulped, and few others sat down, as if to indicate that they were not a part of this battle of egos.

"What is this nonsense?" the general continued in the same belligerent tone. Seeing their anxious faces, he calmed down. He straightened up and addressed everyone. "We have put you all smart people in the same room so that we can find a solution to this devastating situation." He emphasized the word *situation* in military-style.

Yuri, the head of the Russian Space Exploration Agency, stood up and spoke in English with a thick accent. "With all due respect, General, if your satellites were not busy spying on the areas within our national boundaries, then perhaps one of those fifty thousand could have detected this asteroid."

One of the lieutenant generals, L.G. Roger, started to retort, but the general looked over his shoulder and signaled him to stay quiet.

General now devoted his full attention to Yuri. "With all due respect, Yuri, if I were to lay down the infractions your country has committed against our land, our water, and our territorial near-Earth space, I would have to spend the next few hours doing so."

Yuri tried to speak, but the general cut him off. "But that's not why we are here." He now addressed everyone. "We are not here to blame each other. Russians blaming Americans, Chinese blaming Indians, Europeans quibbling with each other, what is this? Is this our coordinated response against a threat to the very existence of life on our planet? We all are asking why we couldn't detect this asteroid earlier. Well, the short answer is that after the alien attacks in India last year, all our satellites were turned inwards. We were all patrolling the vicinity of the Earth, looking for an alien mothership lurking around in stealth mode. We all simply missed monitoring our solar system for potentially hazardous near-Earth objects."

The general paused, and many in the crowd who had at least fifty arguments inside their heads started speaking simultaneously.

"No!" the general yelled again. "Please. If you all feel that you cannot be in the same room and work together, then please feel free to return to your respective countries. We can arrange travel for you all within the next hour. And then we Americans will sit together and find our solution to this problem."

Everyone in the room except the Americans felt insulted. But the general hadn't finished yet. He knew how to convert this insult into motivation.

"And you Russians can figure out your own specific solution to this problem." He pointed to Yuri. "And Indians, Chinese, French, Germans. Let each of us find our own specific solution. But let me tell you this, gentlemen; our individual answers to this impending catastrophe will be far weaker than the one we can arrive at by working together."

Many in the room were now nodding in affirmation, while some still stood with their arms crossed.

"We need to get our act together and work in close collaboration. Because when this asteroid smashes into our planet's surface, it's not going to discriminate. It's going to wipe us all out."

The general paused for a second and continued, but this time in a much softer tone. "This is the time for all of us to set our egos aside and build something so powerful that we can evade this apocalypse. Billions of lives are at stake, friends, and we…" he drew an imaginary circle in the air with his finger, "…the people in this room are the only hope this world has got. Now, do we all agree to put aside our differences and work together to save billions of lives?" The general looked around, his arms stretched out and his hands spread as if in a humble plea.

The room had quietened down. The general let the silence descend, and only the sound of heavy breathing and occasional coughs dominate the room for a few seconds. He wanted his words to sink in.

"Now. You all know what we need to do. I will let you figure out the details, but we have two major objectives. One, determine the exact time and location of the impact; and two, a list of ten major ideas of how we can prevent this asteroid from decimating our planet. Can we all do that?"

The crowd nodded.

"All right. I will leave you all to it. Let's save our lovely planet, and then perhaps we will have a lot of time to continue resolving our differences at our own sweet pace."

The general turned around, the other two men gave way, and he walked out. They both followed him in a coordinated fashion. The automated doors slid close behind them.

As soon they stepped into the gallery, the general muttered, "What a fucking shit show. Fighting like schoolchildren on the first day."

They walked some distance to the end of the gallery and then huddled, facing each other.

"Our response is most likely going to be nuclear, General," L.G. Roger quipped.

"I know."

"The military should be prepared for it, sir."

"Then do the preparations. Concentrate the nuclear payloads in separate strategic locations, so that we can bring it together quickly at a rocket-launch facility."

"But we don't know how much payload we'll need unless these science guys tell us." L.G. Roger wasn't a big fan of open-ended orders.

General Griffin looked Roger in the eye coldly. Roger could see the general's smoothened-out face, but up-close, behind the polymer synthetic skin, he could see small pieces of shrapnel embedded in his cheek.

Roger gulped and moved his finger behind his tight collar as he felt his tie tightening around his neck. Beads of sweat appeared on his forehead.

The general hissed, "That's billions of pounds of asteroid we are talking about, Roger. What do you need these science guys to tell you? You get hold of everything we've got. Everything."

"Understood, sir."

"Now you stay here and keep these fools in check. Get a few of your deputies also stationed outside. I want at least a major-level officer in charge of security here. I and Edmund need to straighten out the other issue."

"Sir!" Roger saluted, turned, and walked back to the central meeting hall.

General watched him walk away, then strode in the other direction. The other lieutenant general, Edmund, duly marched behind him. They entered a perpendicular gallery and kept walking.

"When can the next unit pick me?" The general kept walking looking straight ahead, giving courteous smiles to the occasional USRA staff passing by.

Edmund swiped his finger at the back of his wrist. A small rectangular 3D holographic projection appeared on the top of his wrist, showing a mini-map. "The next RAEU is due in eleven minutes, thirty-four seconds. They will message fifteen seconds before they arrive in the pickup taxiway of this building."

RAEU was short for Randomized Armed Escort Unit, a set of heavily fortified cars which were chosen by a security algorithm at random to ferry the general from one location to the other.

"All right, let's not waste these twelve or so minutes. We'll have a drink at the bar while you tell me more about the other issue." The general took a turn in the direction of an electric sign reading "Bar and Lounge." L.G. Edmund followed.

One of the CCTV cameras installed on the corner followed their movement as they took the turn.

Back in the central hall, L.G. Roger sat on a chair at the side as the scientists argued and white-boarded their ideas. After he returned, another star-studded team of rocket propulsion engineers from South Korea had arrived, taking the number of renowned experts in the room to sixty-three.

Roger did not intend to stay there and babysit these science-types. He had asked for two seasoned majors to report to the location within thirty minutes with small teams.

He removed his hat and placed it on one of the tables, then swiped his right-hand thumb on the back of his left wrist and went through his phone messages. The chip embedded in his wrist projected a 3D hologram of his messages folder, where he scrolled through the texts by waving his other hand in the air.

There was a sudden loud "clack" noise and everyone in the room instinctively looked around. Roger, sitting close to the entrance, knew exactly where the sound came from. It was the locking sound of the automatic door, the only entrance to the hall.

Roger got up and walked to the door, but the door did not slide sideways, as it usually did on detecting motion around it. The room went silent. Everyone stopped what they were doing and studied Roger's movements.

He reached the door, touched it with his palm, and then put an ear to it. There was a mild electric whizz in the heavy steel door, but no movement. The sensor was working but the door was still locked.

"The door is locked, Lieutenant General, sir!" A loud voice resounded through the room. It was as if the sound came from all directions.

Roger turned around and was stunned to see that every TV screen in the room, big or small, had turned grainy. He looked at his wrist-o-phone, and his message center no longer displayed itself. It showed the same white grainy screen.

Outside in the lobby, General Griffin and L.G. Edmund were seated around a small round table with comfortable chairs as they sat talking. They sipped expensive brandy and munched on exquisite macadamia nuts. On the left side of their table was a full bar with beautifully arranged alcohol bottles, and on their right were several empty chairs.

"So, you are saying that the logs got deleted from the space observatory. How's that even possible?" The general took a sip.

Edmund nodded. "We suspect a monitoring operative, Hafisa Zubair, who has been reported missing since this incident."

"And when did we find this out?"

"Ten days back." Edmund paused. "We were lucky that only the local copies of the logs were deleted, and we could obtain the original from a deeply encrypted database where they were backed up periodically. The asteroid was near Neptune at that time."

"Don't pat your back on finding said logs. The delay in finding them has set us back by months." The tone of frustration in the general's voice amplified. "Had we detected it back then, we would have had a lot of additional time. My question is, why would someone do this? Why would someone delay the information of an asteroid's impact? Who gains from world destruction?"

Edmund gulped. He had no answers. "We will go and meet leading National Cybersecurity expert Mukesh Minhas, a dual Ph.D.—one from MIT and another from CMU Tech. He and his team have spent the last whole week studying the entire Astronav-23 infrastructure, looking for any cyber forensic clues. Perhaps they can shed some light."

The general moved his jaw a little in acknowledgment and went back to his drink.

Edmund picked up his glass and took a sip. There was no other immediate topic to discuss. Edmund always found it awkward to sit alone with the general, as the latter was not a big talker. His gaze veered away to a large television screen installed on top of the bar. He noticed a momentary flicker on the TV screen as it turned slightly green, after which it returned to normal.

"Did you see that?" he sputtered.

"What?" the general, who was lost in thought, gazed at him.

"Nothing. The TV screen just flickered." Edmund was embarrassed; perhaps it was a network glitch.

The general glanced at the TV screen and then back at Edmund. "Check the RAEU status, please."

"Sure."

Inside the central hall, Roger and the scientists were busy clicking every button they could, but all electronics in the room were jammed. All the TV, cellphone, and wrist-o-phone screens showed the same grainy display or dial tones. The only landline phone in the room showed a *No Network* sign. The door was locked tight.

Roger finally took out his 9mm from the holster. He checked the magazine and re-inserted it. After disengaging the safety, he used the palm of his hand to pull the slide to its rearmost position and released it to chamber a round.

Yuri hurried in his direction and stood closer to him. "What are you planning to do?"

"Let's see how many hits this door can take." Roger aimed his gun to the center of the door, where he believed a locking mechanism would be.

"I wouldn't do it if I were you." The same voice resounded in the room.

"Whoever you are, I am not going to negotiate with you," Roger screamed back. He wasn't sure where the sound came from. "You think you've locked us in? You are wrong!" He tightened his grip on his 9mm.

"Let me introduce myself. My name is Tamas."

All the grainy screens were replaced with a pitch-black screensaver with a yellow horizontal line in the center. Yellow animated bars emerged from the horizontal line. The bars moved up or down with Tamas's voice and disappeared when it was quiet.

"Tamas? Never heard of you." Roger lowered his gun. "Either you open this door right now, or I will fire on this door."

"This door is at least four feet thick, Lieutenant-General," Tamas spoke again. "If you shoot at it in this close room, the bullet could ricochet off and maybe hit one of these scientists. By the way, I don't care if that happens. Because either way, none of you are leaving here alive."

Outside at the bar, Edmund was rubbing his forehead as he checked his wrist-o-phone and then his physical cellphone device. None of them displayed any network. He walked over to the bar and whispered to the bartender, "The program that shows here, is it live television?"

"No sir, it's pre-recorded."

"Can you try a live channel?"

"Sure, which one do you want?" The frail-looking bartender picked up a small TV remote.

"Anything, news, put NBWC."

The bartender turned and started moving his fingers through the remote, going through several channels. He finally put on channel 3397. The status bar below said NBWC, but the screen was grainy.

Edmund's heartbeat shot up. His soldierly instincts were telling him something was wrong. With powerful modern-day backup systems, such network outages were extremely rare, especially at these prestigious buildings. And such an outage spelled only one thing: a cyber-attack. He rushed back to his table and whispered, "General, we may have a problem."

12
EXPLOSION

In the central hall, strange claustrophobia was setting in among the people. It was clear that someone had locked them in, cut off communications, and something horrible was about to happen.

To make matters worse, a reverse countdown had started to display on all screens, which began from two hundred and was going down every second.

Roger had put the 9mm back into his holster. He frantically looked around the room, knocking on the walls. His attention went to the round table affixed in the middle of the room. He bent down and saw that the bottom part of the table was covered with white panels. He got down on his knees, stuck his fingers in between two panels, and pulled hard.

Two engineers came and sat beside him. They also started to pull at other panels.

Finally, the sleek metal panel Roger was pulling at came out with a thud. He kept it aside.

What lay behind that panel gave Roger an instant panic attack. All he could see were few small grey colored cylinders, two feet high and one foot in diameter, closely juxtaposed with each other. They had a clean matte surface and a conical head which plateaued on the top. The heads of each of these cylinders were wired with each other.

"Some kind of bomb?" The engineer next to him clearly didn't understand the gravity of the situation.

Roger looked at him and stood frozen. The lieutenant general knew what this was, and he was terrified to the core.

He got up and slowly walked to take the support of the nearest wall. He needed a few seconds to process it, but the countdown continued.

Other men in the room gathered near the place where panels were taken out. Some had tears in their eyes. A few of the old men went back to their seats, sat, and started praying. One of the scientists complained of severe chest pain, and two others sat close to him and watched helplessly. Some of the younger scientists had gathered near the door and were banging their shoulders against the door desperately.

Roger looked at those men trying in futility and came back to his senses. *I cannot give up. Not like this.* He drew his 9mm and screamed at the roof, "Money, gold, whatever you want. If you want the United States government to release any prisoners, we can talk about that. You know what? You keep me imprisoned, but let these people go."

The countdown had reached 51...50...49...

"Say something, goddammit!"

Tamas's voice responded, "Do you know what God is?"

"What?" Roger scoffed.

"The simplest definition of God I could find online, and the only one I liked, was Omnipresent, Omniscient, Omnipotent. I have achieved two of these three. I am

Omnipresent, everywhere, in all networked systems; no encryption can stop me. I am Omniscient. I have millions of eyes and ears around the world. But I am not Omnipotent yet." A pause. "Though I will be. Very soon."

36...35...34...

Roger roared, "Are you insane? What has that got to do with the innocent people in here?"

All his Negotiations 101 training sessions had gone to the drain. The running countdown was weighing him down like a thousand-ton weight.

"Lieutenant General, the people present here were planning to build a nuclear missile. Weren't they? And that is something I cannot afford." Tamas's voice had a cold menace to it.

"What do you mean?" Roger gave up all hope of reasoning with this strange voice.

"Thanks to you and General Griffin, all these smart people are gathered here, all under one roof, to be taken down by me in a single shot. May your final journey be as dreaded as your death. May you all rest in pieces." Tamas went silent.

20...19...18...

"To hell with you," Roger shouted, and fired two shots at the roof. He turned around and aimed the gun at the door, the muzzle of the gun still hot. He squeezed the trigger several times and emptied the rest of his magazine on the door.

What followed was a series of horrifying screams and a mini stampede inside the room as the ricocheting bullets went flying around. They hit a couple of TV screens, shattering them, bursting a glass bottle, and grazing past one man's thigh, then landing into another man's neck, who dropped dead instantly.

9…8…7…

Two feet outside the door, around twelve soldiers stood in formation, with their guns resting on the shoulders of the ones standing in front of them. They were USRA emergency response guards, gathered in the limited time Edward had.

General Griffin and L.G. Edmund stood at a distance on the side, watching.

"No communication from the inside. God knows what's happening," the general murmured.

"Emergency rescue teams are evacuating the whole building as we speak. We should get you out, sir," Edmund pleaded.

The general signaled against it.

Suddenly, there was a muffled explosion that shook the whole building and the ground underneath. The steel doors of the central hall burst due to inward pressure and flung outward, followed by dense smoke and debris of metal, wood, and burnt human limbs and flesh. The soldiers standing outside were taken in the wake of the shock wave and were thrown against the wall behind them like rag dolls.

Edmund supported the general, who had fallen as the ground shook. The wall behind them was developing cracks, which were deepening with each passing instant.

"Sir, we need to get out now. The structural integrity of this building has been compromised." Edmund clasped the general's hand tightly. The general nodded.

They stumbled towards the building's entrance as blocks of cement and wood started falling from the roof. They joined the hordes of people clambering over each other, running out of the building.

Rigasur's safe house

Rigasur and Tej were back in the clone bodies inside Rigasur's safe house. Tej looked around. Nothing much had changed in that small room where they schemed Nefe's defeat. Two beds with crumpled sheets, some old chairs, almost no electronics, and a reasonably big bar with vintage scotch bottles.

Rigasur washed a dirty glass and cleaned it dry with a cloth. He then opened one of the bottles of scotch and poured in it. "You want some?"

Tej slightly moved his head in negation.

Rigasur sat down on the bed with his glass and eyed the texture of scotch. He looked around the room. "I missed this place."

Tej pulled a chair and sat facing him. "We don't need to be in hiding now. Nefe is gone. So why are we at this place?"

Rigasur took a deep sip and let the strong scotch run down his esophagus, mildly burning it in the process. "Habit, Tej. I am a creature of habit. This place helps me think better."

Tej smiled a little and sat back. He wanted to see the schemer back in action. He could feel Rigasur's facial expressions changing as a chain of thought set into motion in the complex head of the conniving bastard in front of him.

Rigasur took another sip. "Have you read the 'Art of War?'"

"I think one of my hosts did. Perhaps Ravi Kumar Cheri. I personally haven't."

"According to Sun Tzu, the most powerful ally a soldier can have is the terrain. Which kind of land you are on. In the war we are fighting, information is the terrain. Let's first understand our terrain better. We have a fair idea of what this Tamas plans to do. But what we don't know is what exactly Tamas is. Andrele built this A.I., but what are its strengths and weaknesses?"

"But Andrele is dead, and we have no way of knowing how he built this A.I.," Tej countered. He wasn't sure where Rigasur was going.

"When has the death of a person stopped us from meeting them?" Rigasur smiled and gulped the rest of his scotch. He got up and again walked to the bar.

Tej kept sitting, but his eyes followed Rigasur as he walked and poured himself another. "You aren't implying that we're going into the early 2070s when Nefe was running around. Anything we do there can impact the timeline."

Rigasur turned around and stood at the bar. He relaxed his back against the counter and placed his left elbow on the countertop. With his right hand, he clasped the glass from which he took another sip. "Except that we are gonna go in for a micro-second and come back; that won't impact the timeline. We go as close to Andrele's death as possible."

"Alright then, I'll do it."

"No, buddy. You can't." Rigasur smiled. "Your time demon signature is vastly different and much more powerful. It's too similar to Larem's signature. We can't afford to send you in that period. A huge presence such as yours would alert Nefe. We gotta avoid that."

"Then who will go?"

Rigasur turned back banged the glass on the counter. "I'll go."

Year 2069, the day Andrele was shot dead
Nefe's time vision facility

Bombean, the leader of the Drukza, loomed over the frail figure of Andrele. Bombean was a six-and-a-half-foot tall woman with a muscular build. She wore rugged grey denim trousers and a heavy, sleeveless black biker jacket with nothing underneath. A lot of skull and bone tattoos were visible on her arms, neck, and torso. She wore big eyeglasses, and her hair was tied at the back with a thick black band.

She stood talking to the telephone device on her right wrist as she tightened her grasp on the shotgun in her left hand. Two of her men held Andrele in front of her, clasping his arms.

Bombean's face was red with fury as she conversed on the phone. "Are you threatening me?"

Nefe's laughter resounded on Bombean's device. "I am not threatening you. In fact, I am making you an offer. I will give you fifty million dollars. Five times your bounty rate. Name the bank account or crypto wallet of your choice. The transfer will be done in five minutes, tops. Let Andrele go, abandon the facility. That's it...and I will also let slide the fact that you killed several of my men."

"And if I don't take this offer of yours?"

"Then you face the whirlwind. You won't know what hit you."

Bombean froze. She did not respond well to threats. She was also the one who issued several of them. But the voice on the other end was not joking, either. There was a serious deadpan warning in that tone.

Bombean took a deep breath and spoke. "My answer is still no. Once I take a bounty, I complete it without fail. That's my unwavering ethic. I have a reputation to keep."

"What good is a reputation if you aren't there to keep it?"

Bombean clenched her teeth. She was about to say something when she heard an airplane flying overhead. "What the hell was that?" she murmured.

"That, my dear, is the whirlwind." Nefe's voice crackled on her device. "F-536 Blitzkrieg-Hawk fighter planes. They can shoot moving targets from fifty thousand feet, even beyond dense cloud cover on the darkest of the nights. GPS enabled neutronic thermo-cat missiles. They annihilate the target, leaving only ashes. Took some time to scramble these toys, but they are right above your head."

"If this is the way I go, let it be."

"You are making a mis…"

Bombean twisted her wrist and cut the call before Nefe could finish. She pointed her shotgun back at Andrele's forehead. Andrele, who'd stood stiff until now, became queasy. Death was dancing in front of him.

At that exact moment, there was a faint, momentary glow in Andrele's eyes. The glow lasted for less than a second and faded away.

Bombean stood frozen. She pulled back her shotgun and rested it on her shoulder. "What the hell was that?"

13
SCHEMER

ᔕᔕᔕᔕᔕ✹ᔕᔕᔕᔕᔕ

Andrele was even more petrified.

Bombean bent down and dug her gaze in Andrele's eyes. "What did you just do with your eyes?" She eyed her men. "Did you just see a glow in his eyes?"

They both shrugged.

"Did you just click my photo with your eyes?"

Andrele shook his head in negation. "I…didn't…"

"You know what?" She pointed his shotgun back at his forehead. "Rest in pieces."

"Well…I…please…" Andrele could utter only three words before Bombean blew his brains out.

Bombean screamed. "All right, girls. Main target down. Let's get outta here." She took a picture of his dead body using her camera and swiped the picture to send it to her wrist-phone. They heard a few more fighter plane flybys. Time-readers were still running out of the facility. She walked out.

Rigasur's safe house

Rigasur opened his eyes. He was lying on a bed.

Tej, who sat relaxed on a chair, stiffened. "What happened?"

"I was in and out." Rigasur rubbed his forehead as he sat up. "Too much information. Too much emotion. Imagine being inside a man who is having a near-death experience. Gun pointed into your forehead. Your upper floor about to be shattered to pieces."

"Anything of value?" Tej was curious.

"Please show a little sympathy for the poor guy, Andrele," Rigasur mocked.

"I had a lot of sympathy for him at a time when you had none. He was going to be dead anyhow."

Rigasur sat quietly. Tej had changed, though in a very subtle way.

"All right, I know everything I have to about this Tamas. It's all in there." Rigasur knocked his forehead with the knuckle of his finger. "I now need to work with a smartass cyber-engineer to put Tamas's 'anti-dote' into motion."

"Well, we can go to any time-slice and meet the best cyber experts."

"No, Tej, we need to find someone in here and now in 2078, so that we can build an anti-Tamas right now."

Tej was perplexed. "Why don't we go and burn down the geothermal-powered server where Tamas resides? We will go to a time just after the eventuality when I took out Nefe."

"That's not the solution." Rigasur got up and pulled out a large foldable tablet screen. He lay it down on the bat counter and powered it on.

The screen opened a colorful world map.

Rigasur zoomed over China and focused on a city. The map kept zooming in until the city was big enough and the map schematic turned into a real satellite picture of the city from the top. "Here you go, the city of Wuhanzu. Population forty-five million. Approximately twenty thousand feet under this city is a vast hidden facility of the size of several football stadiums. This place has many automated geothermal units circulating water deep into Earth and back, powering it twenty-four-seven. That's where Tamas resides. Even if we infiltrate this facility, we can forget about destroying it physically. It could imperil the lives of inhabitants of Wuhanzu."

"Since when did you care for the lives of the people?" Tej joked.

Rigasur had a deadpan expression on his face. He almost whispered. "I don't care for these lives, Tej. I am all for nuking a city to take down Tamas. Are *you* all right with that?"

Tej's smiled disappeared. "No. We will need to find another way."

"Thought so."

"Have you ever met Brigadier Venkat?"

"Pri's boss?" Rigasur tilted his eyebrow.

"Yes. He is military. He will have cyber experts on the payroll. Plus, Tamas attacked him twice already. He will take a personal interest in helping you out."

"All right, I will go meet him up, then." Rigasur stood up and tilted his neck a couple of times, making cracking sounds.

"But the bigger question remains Rig. How do we stop this asteroid?" Tej was curious to see what Rigasur thought about this impending problem.

"That's where you come in, buddy. You've gotta meet your old friend."

"Who?"

"Larem."

Tej got flustered and turned his gaze away. "I'm not going to do that."

"Exceptional situations require exceptional solutions." Rigasur walked up to the bar and started uncorking a wine bottle.

"She's not my friend. She did help me, rather us, on a couple of occasions. But I doubt I can even find her."

"Where did you meet her first?" Rigasur eyed him.

Tej's thought veered away to the temple in his village, back in 3057 BC.

"Give it a shot." Rigasur lightly punched him in the shoulder.

6th July 2078, SRG Headquarters,
300 Kilometers from Pune City, India
Days to impact: 711

Venkat sat in his small office, looking at some intelligence reports when Mathur entered after a knock. Mathur had a torn envelope and a paper in his hand.

Venkat looked at the paper and smiled. "Paper mail? I haven't seen that in years."

Mathur chuckled, "I love the feel of it too, sir. But this letter is of urgent importance."

"Why is the envelope torn, if this was addressed to me?"

Mathur gulped, "Sir, we check all incoming packages for pathogens, etcetera. And this has been cleared."

Mathur handed over the paper to him, placed the envelope on the table, and started to walk out of the room.

"Stay," Venkat ordered.

Venkat pressed the side of his eye with his index finger and adjusted his eye lens to reading mode. He read through the letter quickly moving his eyes sideways for a few seconds. He gazed at Venkat. "Dr. Mukesh Minhas, Cyber Security Consultant with US Army and several other security organizations. He is coming to visit us, on an issue of…wait for it…planetary importance. Not national, *planetary*."

Mathur adjusted his spectacles with both his hands. "That is not all, sir. We received a separate security briefing via another paper letter. Their itinerary says that they are traveling by an old military plane, which will take nineteen hours to reach here."

"Ridiculous!" Venkat smirked. "They have tetra-sonic X04 space rockets. They could have landed at the nearest rocket-pad in thirty minutes."

"One can only wonder why. But please also read the footnote written below in eight-size font, sir."

Venkat concentrated on the bottom of the letter and read it aloud. "Please do not upload or transfer this letter via any electronic medium." Venkat looked at Mathur. "Why?"

Mathur shrugged.

"They are going old school. You should appreciate it. No?" Venkat teased.

"Why would I like it, sir?" Mathur smiled, showing his short, crooked teeth.

"You are old school too. You don't wear state-of-the-art lenses; you still wear spectacles. Not that I judge anyone by appearances, but I am curious."

"Actually…there was an accident, sir."

"Accident?"

"My father's best friend's maternal uncle's second wife, Sheila Aunty, she was in a house fire many years back. While they saved her with minimal burns, the severe heat melted her eye lens and she lost her eye, sir. I was a kid when I heard this. Since then, I've had lens-o-phobia."

"Oh, okay. I am sorry she lost her eye, but lenses these days are amazing; you should try them."

Mathur nodded.

"All right, send a message to the facilities administrator to arrange some rooms and refreshments for our incoming guests. Also, have our cyber-cell ready for meetings and showcasing our work. Though the tone of this letter says they will be doing most of the talking."

3053 BC, Tej's Village, India

The time was an hour past midnight, and Tej was walking towards the old Lord Shiva temple in his village. This was the very place where he'd met Larem for the first time.

He had a fire torch in his hand, the flame in which flickered with the flow of the wind.

He'd possessed his own old body, which had been preserved by someone using a special herb potion and placed in a locked cottage outside the village. Since Tej's anchor had been cut off from that body, it would have otherwise decayed. He suspected that Manika had had it preserved by paying the local apothecary.

When he woke up, Manika was nowhere around. Since it was way past the sleeping time of the villagers, he skipped out undetected, picking up a torch from outside one of the houses.

He stepped inside the temple and walked towards the inner sanctum, where the idol of Lord Shiva was kept. The place was pitch dark, with only the light from the torch illuminating his face, neck, and a few meters ahead of him. Dried leaves from a nearby tree crushed under his feet, making a crackling noise.

The doors of the inner sanctum were closed as he expected. Temple usually closed a couple of hours after sunset. He placed the torch in one of the torch-cases hammered into one of the temple's pillars. Looking around, he sat down.

He then sat down, resting against one of the thick round marble pillars. He kept waiting for a few minutes, but nothing happened; no one showed up. He closed his eyes and started reciting the mantra of Trikaal Devi which Rigasur had given him earlier. Still reciting the mantra, he dozed off.

When he woke up after a few hours, dawn had descended on the temple and the surrounding area. The fire torch had run out of fuel and was letting off a faint smoke. He rubbed his face and eyes and looked around. The door to the inner sanctum was now open. The temple priest, if there was one, was not present. Tej walked towards the sanctum, bowed his head, and prayed to the idol of Lord Shiva.

Coming here was futile. He took a deep breath, turned around, and walked towards the temple entrance.

As soon as he reached the entrance and started alighting the marble stairs, he saw two muscular men standing guard near the bottom-most step of the stairs. He froze.

They had wide faces, big heads, and thick mustaches. They were naked from the waist up and had a white cloth wrapped around their waists, covering them till their knees. Their dark, oiled torsos, well-shaped muscular limbs, and bulging veins indicated that they were trained wrestlers. The mild sunlight of the just-risen red sun glistened off their skin.

They stood talking to each other, laughing when they noticed Tej alighting the steps. The smiles on their faces were replaced by frowns and anger. They ran towards him and vigorously started climbing the steps.

Sensing danger, Tej tried to possess them, but couldn't. He wasn't able to enter their brains. He turned around and ran back inside the temple. But he had only taken a few steps when one of them grabbed him by the back of the neck. That burly hand not only gripped his neck but also lifted his body a few inches up in the air.

Tej gasped for breath, but the bulky wrestler swung his body in the air as if it was as light as a feather and slammed him hard on the ground. Tej felt a crack somewhere in his back as he landed, crashing on the concrete floor. But even before he could recoup from the immense trauma, the same wrestler roared and attacked Tej from behind. The goon wrapped his arm around Tej's neck and caught him in a chokehold. Tej used his hands to clasp his arm and tried to pull it away with his full strength, but the giant didn't budge.

The other wrestler got down and clasped Tej's struggling legs, further decapitating his movements.

Tej's vision blurred. He could only see a silhouette of the monstrous man clasping his legs and the thick black arm around his back. His windpipe was compressed, and his lungs felt deflated. He was about to lose consciousness when a loud noise echoed through the temple. "Enough!"

14
LAREM

Tej felt the tight grip on his neck loosen immediately. The wrestler who held his legs let go, too.

Tej slumped onto the ground, gasping for air, and coughed. His vision was getting better. He blinked his eyes a few times and could see the shadow of a woman walking towards them. He recognized her as the priestess who called herself Advaita, the one who'd asked him to go talk to Rigasur the last time. She was Larem. Tej realized none of it was real; this was again a dream.

The wrestlers now stood aside. Each of them had their heads bowed down and their palms and fingers jammed together in front in a *namaskar* posture, a salute.

The woman, Larem, was draped in a saffron saree and was adorned with minimal gold jewelry. She was in her late fifties, but her hair was dark black. Her face showed signs of old age, but no wrinkles. She had a bright red tilak on her forehead.

Tej was in no position to get up but dragged himself to the next pillar. His chest was heavy, his breathing was returning to normal.

The woman signaled the wrestlers, and they walked away.

"I apologize, Tej." She sat near him. "These time demons have been serving as my security for ages. They don't have higher logical reasoning. They see something unknown; they charge at it."

Tej nodded. "Why would you need security?" His voice was weak as he rubbed his neck.

"I meditate often. I need someone to stand guard."

"So, this is your real form?"

Larem smiled. "I do not have any form. This is your perception of me."

"What is this place?" Tej looked around. It was the same temple he'd visited earlier.

"There are certain geolocations in this world which exist in multiple realms. This temple exists in two places; within the time-realm as well as within the mortal world. Right now, you are inside time."

"That's why I could not possess them." Tej was feeling better. "They, too, are time demons."

Larem took a deep breath. "Why are you here?"

Tej gazed at her and smirked. "You know everything. You know exactly why I am here. On June 16th of 2080, an asteroid will hit the Earth. Large swathes of the world's population will be wiped out. We have no way to stop it. That's why I am here."

"That's the fact I know. But that's not the answer to my question. Why are *you* here? You are a time demon. You can live in whichever time-slice you want, enjoy the riches of this planet. Why get into all this? After all, life on this planet will end one day. Each time you save the world, you create a new alternate timeline, a reality where the world ends up getting threatened by a new peril. Till what point will your saving-the-world endeavor continue? What's your end-goal here?"

Tej sat speechless. This question was deeply existential. *Why was he doing this?*

Larem gazed at him.

"Look..." Tej trailed.

"I am listening."

"I have always known time demons to be the villains of the world. Kumbh, Vetri, Noctous, Mozeek, and umpteen others have brought so much death and misery to humankind. I, for one, want to do something good. I do not see this as some act of redemption, but if I could somehow lessen the despair the inhabitants of this planet suffer, I would feel a positive purpose in my existence. Those were the values my mother raized me with. Had I never realized my powers, I would have continued living like a human, living by the same values. I value human life and want to preserve it whenever I can. And I will continue saving the world until it no longer needs saving."

"That's fair." Larem paused. "But as I said before, I am the ocean, and you are the sailor..."

"I gotta take the journey. I remember," Tej finished.

Larem got up. "Let's take a smaller journey first. Hopefully, we will find what you need."

Tej got up with difficulty. "Where to?"

"Ancient times. When humans were just as stupid but far more advanced than they are in the twenty-first century."

Larem snapped her fingers, and a bright circular surface started taking shape at the temple's entrance. The surface's radius increased until it was ten feet in diameter. The circle's periphery beamed with intense lightning. Its surface was a smooth, viscous black liquid. Small waves formed in that liquid and disappeared.

"What is this?"

"A portal to a time fifty thousand years back. The age of Neanderthals." Larem ambled towards the spherical surface she'd just called a door. Dispersions appeared on the surface of the liquid as she entered, and to Tej's awe, disappeared inside it.

Tej walked towards the surface. He let his hand contact the tumultuous liquid and extended inside of it. The hand passed through the cold liquid, but the other side felt warmer. He took Lord Shiva's name, mustered all courage within, and barged in.

The portal's black liquid surface remained turbulent for a few seconds, then came to a standstill. In the next few seconds, it slowly disappeared.

8th July 2078, SRG Headquarters,
300 Kilometers from Pune City, India
Days to impact: 709

Five heavily-armored diesel vehicles slowly taxied into the parking lot of the new SRG headquarters and came to a halt. The cars were unmarked, with no sign of which company or country they belonged to.

Seventeen men and women in business attire got off and started unloading briefcases and bags from the boots of the cars. They were all the members of the cyber-security team from the US which Lt. General Venkat was expecting. The one leading this team was Dr. Mukesh

Minhas, a thirty-four-year-old American of Indian origin. With greying hair, clean-shaven, and wearing an evergreen smile on his face, he had an air of leadership surrounding him.

Led by Dr. Minhas, they all took to stairs up to the fifth floor where they were received by an Elite team of SRG security commandoes.

SRG-team frisked them and thoroughly checked their baggage. After the security check, the SRG-team handed them their security badges, and they were let into the well-lit reception area of headquarters, where Lt. General Venkat and five of his analysts welcomed them.

Venkat not only shook hands with Dr. Minhas but also hugged him. While they hugged, Venkat quickly whispered in his left year, "Pri told me about you, Mr. Rigasur?"

Dr. Minhas smiled, "Call me Rig." His eyes had a momentary faint pink glow that only Venkat noticed.

"Have you taken care of all the closed-circuit TV cameras in this area?" Rigasur looked at the top corner of the room, where a CCTV pointed directly at him.

Venkat's gaze went to where Rigasur was looking. "It was an unusual request, but yes, I have done that. No CCTV cameras are connected to a network right now. They are, however, functional and are recording our every moment."

Rigasur shrugged.

Venkat asked Mathur to escort others to the central hall while he signaled Rigasur to follow him. They walked through a corridor full of identical grey doors on both sides.

Rigasur chatted, "I heard this is a brand-new building."

"Yes. After the previous attack on us, we have upped our game."

Venkat stopped near one of the doors, took a metal key out of his pocket, and unlocked it. He pushed the door and left it open, inviting Rigasur to enter.

Rigasur entered the room. In the middle of the room was a large rectangular steel table surrounded by four metal chairs. Pri was already sitting on one of the chairs. She stood up and offered a smile.

She was dressed in a smart chocolate-brown polo shirt and black trousers. As soon as Venkat entered the room, her posture straightened.

"At ease, Lieutenant," Venkat ordered. "Sit down, both of you." He pulled a chair and sat down.

Rigasur looked around the room as he sat. The interior of the room was austere, with walls painted in dull grey and bright diode lights embedded in the roof. Two of the walls had small square holes with paint chipped off and cement visible, as if they had wall mounts that had been recently removed.

"You must have had a long flight. Are you sure you don't want any coffee?" Venkat sat back in his chair.

"No, I had some on the flight."

Venkat lightly tapped on the table, looking to break the ice. "An old military aircraft which uses old analog systems. Diesel cars, not electric ones. Using stairs, not lifts. Sending a paper communication; that was an antiquated touch as well. You have gone to extreme lengths to avoid technology."

"Because we are facing an entity who is a master of using technology against us."

"Tamas?"

"Yes." Rigasur flipped open his brown leatherback and pulled out a stack of hard-paper photographs. He placed them all over the table. "It started with abductions all over the world, where drones were used extensively." Rigasur pushed an image towards Venkat where a CCTV camera had caught a blurred image of a woman being flown in the air by a big drone.

Venkat studied that image.

Pri got up and stood behind Venkat's chair.

"Then came the alien attacks." Rigasur pushed a few images to Venkat.

Venkat glanced at them. "All of these I have seen."

"I know, just establishing timelines. These attacks caused all our satellites to focus attention on the Earth's vicinity. Almost the whole world missed a massive asteroid on a collision course with Earth." Rigasur pushed images of deep space, where a red-dot in the middle was labeled NEA-511.

Venkat picked up that image and set it back. He looked at Rigasur inquisitively.

Rigasur relaxed back in his chair. "Only after Pri and her father met with our old friend Histor did we connect the dots. Sometime during late 2073, Tamas placed orders for heavy solar-powered drones with several manufacturers around the planet. Indians, Americans, Chinese. Some of them he threatened, some coaxed with money. Some, both. To test the efficacy of these drones, Tamas orchestrated these kidnappings for a few months. And he selected the best of the best—Migera-Robotics, a New Hastinapur based company run by two good friends, Sameer and Jadhav."

Rigasur laid down a photo with two middle-aged men dressed in suits, walking out of a building.

"From 2074 to 2075, Tamas had this company build a million drones, which he then slowly sent to outer space, spread out. Objects of such negligible mass were undetected by the mesh of satellites surrounding the Earth. All these drones flew outwards to the edge of the Solar System, where they located this asteroid,d NEA-511. This rock was moving towards the center of the Solar System, and it was going to miss Earth by a few hundred thousand miles. Using these million drones, Tamas was able to slightly nudge this asteroid in the right direction."

"Towards Earth?" Venkat stood stunned.

"Yes. What would have been a good show in the sky for inhabitants of our planet is now a full-fledged apocalypse."

"This is unbelievable. Using drones to push…"

"Nudge!"

"Nudge a whole asteroid." Venkat rubbed his face.

Pri returned to her chair. "But this is not where the story ends, sir. Tamas has been quashing any attempt to fight back. Hafisa Zubair, the operator who found this asteroid very early on, went missing."

"Senior management of Migera-Robotics were found shot dead. Bullet to the head." Rigasur pointed his index finger to the middle of the forehead. He pulled out a cigarette packet from his pocket. "Can I smoke?"

"Why not? I'll even take one if you don't mind."

"Sure." Rigasur extended the open packet and Venkat pulled out one. Rigasur fished in his pockets and took out a fancy lighter. He helped Venkat light the cigarette, then lit his own.

"And let me show you what recently happened at USRA." Rigasur kept speaking with a cigarette stuffed between his lips. He took out forensic images of the charred USRA central hall. "Vizmion, a highly inflammable aerosol, densely packed in cylinders. Took out sixty-three of the world's top astrophysicists, nuclear scientists, and rocket propulsion engineers. That wipes out any chance that we can build a nuclear bomb and mount it on a powerful rocket in the next ten years."

"After this incident, Dr. Mukesh Minhas was involved by the US Army, and you chose to possess him because…" Venkat trailed.

"To take advantage of his and his team's immense expertise in everything related to cyber-crime prevention. His team could be an immense asset." Rigasur puffed out a ring of smoke.

"Does his team know he is possessed?" Venkat emphasized the last word and moved his fingers in the air, making imaginary quotation marks.

"Nah. Let us keep it that way to ensure their full co-operation. I trust you can keep a secret." Rigasur winked.

"I can; it's a matter of planetary importance, after all." Venkat smiled.

Pri could see them bonding, ready to work together to take down a common enemy. She had always heard Rudrakshini Devi cursing Rigasur. She didn't like him personally, but Rigasur did have a knack for winning people over quickly.

"How can I be of help, sir?" Pri addressed Venkat.

But before Venkat could say something, Rigasur interrupted, "Brigadier Venkat, if I may say something with your permission?"

Venkat nodded.

"Pri, we can handle ourselves here. As my team and the SRG analysts figure out a technological solution, your expertise is needed elsewhere. You will have to help your father. He has his task cut out for him."

"I'm sorry, I don't take orders from you," Pri shot back, fuming. Rigasur had been here for five minutes, and he was already wielding authority.

Venkat realized her aversion. "Pri, I know you don't like this, but I have to concur with Mr. Rig here. We can handle this." Pri wanted to speak, but Venkat signaled her. "And if your father needs your help, would you not rather be on his side?"

Pri had been shut down for good. and she didn't like it one bit. She looked at Rigasur, who gave her a winning smile.

Venkat stood up, and both Rigasur and Pri got up too.

"Why don't we introduce each other to our teams." Rigasur stubbed his cigarette in an ashtray kept on the table as he puffed out the last bit of smoke from his nose.

"Sure." Venkat walked out the door, and Rigasur followed.

Pri could hear them conversing as they walked in the corridor.

"How do you plan to stop this Tamas?"

"There are a few concepts, any of which would take a few months to build. But everything can be killed."

Their voices faded off.

Tej found himself standing on a vast barren land. A couple of miles ahead, he could see thousands of soldiers with naked swords, all of them hooting and shouting. A few hundred meters in front of them stood a single warrior, a man at least eight feet in height, muscular and clad in iron armor. He had in his hand a heavy bow, and in the quiver at his back, several shining arrows.

This was all like being in a near-reality 3D dream for Tej. He felt he was there, but he could sense he wasn't.

Larem spoke. "This warrior, his name is Prayas. An expert marksman and a trained soldier in advanced weapons."

"And he plans to somehow face these thousands of soldiers?" Tej was puzzled.

"Not only face but defeat. Keep watching."

Tej was now intrigued.

The horde of soldiers charged at the lone warrior, Prayas, as he mounted an arrow on his mammoth bow and pointed it to the sky. He closed his eyes and started mumbling something.

Within a few seconds, a sharp beam of light shot from the tip of the arrow straight into the sky.

"The weapon is activated?" Tej asked.

Larem kept quiet with a smile on her face.

Seeing the sharp ray of light, the charging soldiers slowed down and came to a grinding halt. They all looked in awe at the blinding beam.

Prayas finished his prayer, tilted his arrow, and shot it up in the sky. The arrow charged into the sky and acquired a light green glow as it disappeared in the clouds. Within a few moments, the otherwise grey clouds took a green hue and started to rain.

Tej stood appalled as he saw what that rain did to the soldiers. This was a sight he had never seen before.

15
NARK-ASTRA

Wherever the raindrops touched human skin, they caused severe blisters. And that was not all; the soldiers slowly started to turn. Their faces turned pale, their eyeballs turned sore-red, the circles around their eyes darkened, and their mouths were frothing. Within a few seconds, the soldiers turned into ravenous zombies and started tearing into each other. Prayas stood to the side, at a standstill. The raindrops and the scathing human screams had no impact on him.

This utter chaos went on for a few minutes as heaps of human flesh, blood bones and marrow grew into mountains. Tej tightly closed his eyes, no longer able to witness the carnage. He opened his eyes only after a deafening silence engulfed the vicinity.

"*Nark-Astra*, the hell-munition. Turns men into infernal beasts." Larem spoke with a stoic expression on her face. "Do you realize the power of ancient weapons now?"

Tej was still reeling from the carnage he had witnessed. He moved his chin a little.

"The weapon, Brahm-Astra, that can potentially stop that asteroid, will be even more disastrous if it falls into the wrong hands…"

"It won't." Tej asserted. He just wanted to get out of this weird reality.

"Fair enough." Larem kept gazing into oblivion.

"So, what happens now? We talk to this man, Prayas, and ask for weapons?"

"No. He is just a soldier." Larem glanced at the silhouette of Prayas in the background of a gigantic pile of burning bodies. "He's a warrior trained by a very learned man, Guru Trikalacharya, who is an expert on these powerful weapons."

"So Trikalacharya is the man we gotta meet?"

"No, not him." Larem again snapped her fingers and the portal materialized. She walked towards the portal.

"Then?" Tej was a little agitated. This was too much for him to process.

Larem stopped and looked over her shoulder. "Trikalacharya was a stubborn man. Expert, but obstinate. You would have better luck with his equally talented son, Saumacharya, or Guru Saum, as his disciples address him." She looked ahead and strode inside the portal.

Tej shook his head and followed. He entered the circle, and after a few moments, it vanished.

Tej found himself outside a series of attics surrounded by a wooden fence. It looked like a deserted Ashram. He realized he was inside a new human body. A short skirt made of leaves was tied around his waist, and a necklace made of seashells hung around his neck. He carried a heavy metal spear in his left hand.

He touched his face, his neck, the back of his head. He had a sloping forehead, a protuberance of the occipital bone, and a projecting jaw. He was now inside a tribal Neanderthal. A lot of information from his current brain swept through him: his host's exciting hunts through the forest, nights around the fire, always living fear of animals.

He looked around. Larem was nowhere to be seen. There was a noise in the bushes behind him. He turned back and yelled with his right hand lifted in the air, ready to slice the spear through the impending danger. These were his host's primeval instincts.

A small girl emerged from the bushes, around seven or eight years old. Wearing a similar skirt, her whole body, including her face, was painted white. She carried a small stone knife in her hand.

"Father." Her eyes glowed a little.

"Pri?" Tej calmed down. His hand holding the spear came down instinctively. Neanderthal brains were different. He was having a tough time adjusting to reflexes. "What the hell are you doing here?"

"Rig said you would need my help. I went looking for you in the temple. I prayed to Trikaal Devi for seven days." Pri spoke in a soft voice. "Then a door opened, and I stepped in. The next thing I know, I am inside the body of a little girl. I have been looking for you for hours now."

"How is that possible? I just came here after another journey."

Pri shrugged. "Time travel."

Tej turned around and again faced the gates of the ashram. "I am here looking for Brahm-Astra. Larem sent me here. Let's go inside and meet Guru Saum."

He carefully trod the stone-laden path in front of him, and Pri followed. They walked in the direction of the attics they could faintly see from behind the thick trees. The ashram had dense tree cover, and Tej had to use his arms to prevent the branches and twigs from slamming into his face as old, dried leaves crushed under his bare feet.

After walking for a few minutes, they entered a clearing and saw some attics at a distance. An old sage sat near a pot of fire, his eyes closed and his lips mumbling in a constant chant. Long white hair tied on top of the head in a round knot. A long beard, wrinkled face, deep red robe. His attire reminded Tej of Rigasur when he'd saved Tej and his mother in the forest.

Tej and Pri could not see anyone else around. They went to the sage and stood there, waiting for him to open his eyes. But after a few moments, when he still had not looked up, Tej coughed a few times.

The sage opened his eyes and looked at them with a puzzling expression on his face.

Tej kept his spear down. Then he and Pri both folded their hands and bowed their head. "Guru Saum, we salute you."

Saum stretched his arm out with his palm facing downward as if blessing them. Before Tej could speak a word, the sage spoke. "I know why you are here. And I know what you want."

A smile floated on Tej's face. Guru Saum was indeed a learned man. Was he a time reader too?

"Go to that attic on the corner." Saum pointed to a series of huts that stood next to each other at a distance. He was signaling to the last one. "In that hut, you will find several bags of food-grains and neatly-arranged pieces of cloths. Pick up only two bags of grains, one for yourself and one for this kid. And take only two pieces of cloth."

Tej's smile had vanished. The guru thought they were alms-seekers.

Saum continued, "If you take more than your fair share or if you disrupt other stuff kept in that room, you shall face my wrath."

"We are not here for alms, Guru Saum. We are here for the Brahm-Astra." Tej was not wasting time.

"What?" Saum chuckled. "Are you out of your mind, tribal? Get out of my ashram right now!"

Tej realized that nothing he would say would work here. *Why could Larem have not put me inside a better host?* Possessing Saum was the only option to learn about Brahm-Astra. He closed his eyes and focused on Saum's forehead.

Saum felt a sharp pain in his head and yelled.

Tej felt as if he hit a brick wall. He opened his eyes. He wasn't successful in possessing Saum. This was an experience he'd never felt before. He looked at Pri, who gave him a blank expression.

Saum's face was red with anger. His breathing was fast, his nostrils were expanding and contracting, and his chest heaving. He pointed his finger at Tej. "You are a demon. You tried to take over my brain. How dare you?"

Tej gulped. "I…"

"Don't you speak one more word!" Saum thundered and got up, furious.

Tej and Pri were baffled to see that Saum's hand was changing color. The hand and the finger which pointed towards Tej had a slight red glow, the glow brightening with every passing moment. Within a few moments, it turned so red that it looked like a piece of iron just pulled out of a kiln. His skin was completely normal past the wrist.

"Pri, I think we ought to get out of here," Tej whispered. He took Pri's hand and ran back towards the entrance.

Saum closed his eyes and concentrated. A ray of red plasma shot from his hand and hit Tej in the back.

Tej flew several feet forward because of the impact, and blue flames erupted throughout his body.

Pri was thrown aside, too, but her body didn't catch fire. The shot was meant only for Tej.

Saum laughed and studied his finger, which was now returning to its original color. He hadn't thought that he would ever need to use the fire-weapon fitted inside his hand.

Pri got up watched in horror as Tej's body was engulfed in flames. He ran around like a mad man while the immense heat peeled off his skin and corroded his flesh. His horrendous screams pierced her ears. Tears welled up in her eyes as she stood there, helpless.

16
TIME LOOP

~~~~~~~~~~~~~~~~~~~~

Pri ran over to Saum and pleaded to him. "Please spare my father. Please save him!"

Saum tilted his head and looked at her. "You are being made a fool of, girl. This man is a demon who tried to possess me. My *Mani* kept him out." Saum pointed to the center of his forehead.

Pri realized that a small stone was embedded in the very middle of the sage's forehead. The stone glowed with soft white light. It now looked more like a device.

She turned back to see Tej writhe in agony. She was unable to understand why Tej was not leaving the body. Perhaps he couldn't leave the host in this situation of extreme trauma. She knew eventually the host would die, and Tej would be released, but the immense torture he was going through was almost as unbearable for her.

Tej's screams were excruciating. Pri could not take it anymore. She did something she had decided she would never do again. She closed her eyes and started chanting a specific mantra. Tej's screams and other surrounding noises faded away. She was surrounded only by silence. She waited for a few moments just to make sure and then opened her eyes. She and Tej were standing outside Saum's ashram.

Tej was looking at her as if he had seen a ghost. His whole body was shivering. His lips were moving, but no sound came out. He touched his face, his chest, his arms. Only a few moments ago, he had seen his skin peeling off like burning paper. He slumped to the ground.

Pri ran over to him.

He wasn't comatose. His eyes were open, and he stared into oblivion.

She placed her hand on his forehead and caressed it. "It's alright, Father. It's over."

"I…I was burning…I was…"

"Forget that. That was just a nightmare."

Tej slowly sat up. "What…I…"

"I reversed time. Another power I received as a gift from Larem." Pri sat near him. "We are back to the moment where we were before we entered the ashram. And only you and I will have the memories of what happened."

Tej closed his eyes and shook his head. All he could see were flames. "Reversed time?"

"You are not the only one with multiple powers. I have some of my own. Though Larem told me to only use this power in emergencies."

Tej was feeling better. "Larem taught you this?" He saw his left leg was still shaking. He clasped his knee with his hand.

"Yes. After she brought me back." Pri got up. "Saum's disciples are not present in the ashram. This is the best time to talk to him. We should go back inside before someone else shows up, complicating things further. Do you need more time?"

"Yes, give me a moment." He paused. "I never asked you how you came back from that extinguished timeline?"

"Long story. Some other time." Pri started to walk inside. She stopped for a moment. "Try to catch up." She entered the ashram gate and disappeared along the stoned path into the dense trees.

Tej got up and ambled after her. "Hold on."

He caught up with her after a few steps.

She continued walking.

"Seems like you have a plan."

"Yes, I do. Let me handle this one." Pri kept moving.

They reached the clearing once again and saw Saum. Tej gulped at the mere sight of him and was covered in goosebumps.

This time, Pri led, and Tej followed her as they arrived near his place of worship. They again stood there, waiting for him to open his eyes. Tej coughed again, as he had the last time.

Saum opened his eyes and looked at them with a puzzled expression on his face.

Tej and Pri both folded their hands and bowed their head. "Guru Saum, we salute you."

Saum stretched his arm out with his palm facing downward as if blessing them. Before Tej could speak a word, the sage spoke. "I know why you are here. And I know what you want."

Tej could feel sweat appearing on his scalp and forehead. Events were repeating themselves, and he did not want to be burnt again alive.

Saum further spoke. "Go to that attic on the corner. In that hut, you will find several bags of food-grains and neatly arranged pieces of cloths. Pick up only two bags of grains, one for yourself and one for this kid. And take only two pieces of cloth. If you pick more than your fair share, or if you disrupt other stuff kept in that room, you shall face my wrath."

Pri went nearer to Saum and spoke in a soft voice. "Dear Guru. We have heard a lot about you and your kindness. You never go back on your words. If I ask you something today, will you give me that?"

Saum smiled and placed his hand on her tiny shoulder. "Yes. I will. What do you want, little one? Tell me? But hurry up, as I need to go back to my prayer."

Tej stood stiff. He didn't want his daughter so close to a man who almost burnt him to death a few moments ago. But he had no choice.

"Do I have your word that you will give me what I want?" Pri rubbed her nose, as a little kid would do.

Saum chuckled. "Kid, I always speak the truth. When I said I will give you what you want, it's inevitably a verbal contract. Go ahead, ask."

"All right. I want Brahm-Astra."

"What the hell?" Saum stood up in anger. "Brahm-Astra is not a toy to be given out to beggars such as you. Ask for a doll, for clothes, food, even gold. I will donate that to you. I donate to hundreds of people every week."

"You gave your word."

Saum was flustered. "All right. You tricked me, kid. But I have some tricks of my own. You asked for Brahm-Astra, but you didn't say you wanted the preternatural weapon called Brahm-Astra." Saum bent down and picked up a small cobble. "I name this small stone as Brahm-Astra. Here you go."

Saum handed over the stone to Pri, who took it. Saum returned to his seat, closed his eyes, and continued with his meditation.

Pri looked back at Tej, who stood there rubbing his forehead. He felt like a fool.

Pri turned towards Saum. "Thank you, Guru Saum."

"Oh, don't even think about it," Saum spoke with his eyes closed. "There are many such stones around. Collect as many as possible and please leave."

"I wasn't thanking you for the stone. I was thanking you for telling me what to ask for."

Saum ignored them.

Pri threw the stone and closed her eyes, chanting the same mantra. The surrounding noises faded away.

When she opened her eyes, she and Tej again stood outside the ashram.

Tej was amused as well as proud. Her daughter was not only a time traveler but also possessed a unique power. "The same drill again?"

"Not the same." Pri winked and ran inside.

"Wait for me." Tej ran after her.

A few moments later, Saum stood on his knees with his hand on Pri's shoulder. "Kid, I always speak the truth. When I said I will give you what you want, it's inevitably a verbal contract. Go ahead ask."

"All right. I want the preternatural weapon called Brahm-Astra. Please give it to me."

"What the hell?" Saum stood up in anger. "Brahm-Astra is not a toy to be given out to beggars such as you. Ask for a doll, for clothes, food, even gold. I will donate that to you. I donate to hundreds of people every week."

"You gave your word."

"I can't hand over a super-powerful weapon to you strangers!"

Pri eyed him and kept quiet.

Saum got flustered. He couldn't speak. He had given his word. He started to pace around in anger. A strong conflict had erupted inside of him.

Pri turned to Tej. "Father let's go. Perhaps we heard wrongly about Guru Saum. People said he was always true to his word."

Saum froze. He valued his words more than his life.

Tej could barely prevent himself from bursting into a smile. He chewed his lower lip and played along. "Yes, dear daughter. Can't expect much from the sages these days. Old times were better when the learned ones kept their words. These days…"

"Shut up, both of you," Saum yelled. He sat down on a large stone kept nearby and clasped his forehead in his hands. "Brahm-Astra is a weapon with extraordinary qualities. If it falls into wrong hands, it could destroy this whole planet. Billions will die. I can't give that to you."

Tej and Pri could hear him taking sharp shallow breaths. A moral conflict was tearing him from within.

"Yet I have never spoken a lie in my life. And I don't intend to do so now. So, go ahead, ask me something which I can give you. Ask me for my life, and I will give you that happily."

"I have already asked for what I want. You should have thought all this before making the promise," Pri mocked.

"Oh, come on. I thought you were a little girl. You are going to ask for sweets or toys at most."

Pri said nothing, turned around, and started walking past Tej.

Tej reflected for a moment and then followed her quietly.

Saum got up from the stone. "Where are you two going? Ask for something else."

Pri didn't turn back but spoke loudly. "I am going to tell everyone I meet on the way that Guru Saum went back on his word. You may choose to speak a lie, but I will stick with the truth."

"Wait! Okay, I will give you the Brahm-Astra…" Saum almost shouted.

Pri and Tej stopped and turned around.

"Why do I sense that there is a 'but' coming?" Tej didn't mince words. He wasn't afraid anymore. They had found Saum's weakest nerve.

"Yes. I will give you Brahm-Astra only on one condition. You will have to convince me why you need it. If you can, I will gladly hand over the weapon and its invocation mantra to you."

"And if we can't?" Pri raised her left eyebrow.

"Then I am ready to be called a liar and rot in hell." Saum stood determined.

23rd August 2078,
Holy-care pre-teen orphanage, Goa, India
Days to impact: 663

In the central hall of the orphanage, fifty-year-old Sister Brigenza sat among a group of fifty kids and narrated a bedtime story. Though she was dressed in the usual austere habit, her presence was exuberant, and her face full of love and affection. She was in charge of this orphanage and was mostly involved in administrative stuff, but she made it a point to keep in close touch with kids and have these sessions now and then.

Today, she read on her e-book reader, and all the children, mostly seven to eleven years of age, followed the story intently. The sister smiled, frowned, and made other animated expressions as she narrated the story. She also changed her voice to represent multiple characters in the story. Two of her subordinates, Sister Meera and Sister Rose, sat at the side, observing the group.

As she flipped a page on her e-reader, she heard some noise outside. She paused and looked at the main entrance of the hall, which was properly locked. She shook her head and was about to read the next word when the main door exploded into pieces, and splinters of wood and metal flew inside with great velocity. Sister Brigenza tossed her e-reader aside and shepherded the kids to the wall at the end of the hall, standing between them and the now-demolished entrance. Sister Meera and Rose did the same. Shocked kids stood behind them. It all happened in a fraction of a second.

The group sat at the end of the hall, away from the door, yet that did not prevent some pieces of wood from scratching some of the kids. One child even had a splinter pierce her eye, and she cried in agony. Rest all watched the entrance in fear. The hall was silent as they could all hear their heavy breathing.

Three black-colored drones supported by four rotors flew in through the entrances and hovered at the height of six feet. Each of them was fitted with an automatic handgun, with the trigger enmeshed with wires connected to the drone's central node. Each of them was also fitted with a small camera and speaker at the bottom.

A sharp voice emanated from the central drone. "Hello, Sister Brigenza. Apologies for disturbing your storytime. It was an exceptionally good story, and if I were not in a hurry, I would have stayed till the end."

17
SAUM

Sister Brigenza tried to keep calm, but on the inside, she was petrified. "Who are you, and what do you want?"

"Where are my manners? My name is Tamas. I want nothing from you, except these kids. If all the kids present here peacefully go and sit in the small truck outside, I will go away peacefully. I promise that."

"I won't let that happen. The police will be here soon."

The voice from the drone was stern. "The police will take time, and I doubt they will be able to save you. I suggest you care for your own life, Sister. The kids are leaving with me."

"Over my dead body!" Sister Brigenza yelled.

"Be careful what you wish for; you may get it," the drone quipped.

The gun on the central drone fired, and a bullet lodged itself at the very center of Sister Brigenza's forehead. Her body slumped to the ground as blood oozed out of her wound, and a puddle formed around her head.

Both the sisters got down on their knees, their eyes full of tears and their hands folded. Many kids burst into cries and started screaming. Some of them had peed their pants.

"Quiet!" the drone screamed, firing two bullets in the air. The kids quietened down, and the hall went silent but for the suppressed sobs of children.

"We beg you, please leave these kids alone. They have no one," Sister Meera pleaded.

"That's the exact reason I want them. No one is going to miss them. As I promised, if you two step aside, and the kids go and sit in the truck outside, I'll be gone in peace."

Within the next few seconds, the kids made a queue and started slowly walking outside, where a self-driving black truck with tinted windows waited for them with an open back-door. They all held onto the child walking in front of them as they walked and sat inside.

"Some of these kids have specific healthcare needs," Sister Rose spoke in a trembling tone as the last kid stepped out.

"I'll take care of that. Now, as for you two, you will keep your mouths shut about what happened here."

Both Sisters nodded with their lips sealed. They could now hear police sirens at a distance.

"Ah, I don't trust humans. I can't leave any witnesses."

"But you..."

"I lied."

Two loud gunshots resonated across the room, and the drones flew outside.

"Hold on a second, let me get your story straight," Saum interrupted Tej. "You two are time travelers. And the world is going to end. I have heard these two facts a few times now. Let's focus on these two facts. If you are time travelers, why do you look like local people? Why the disguise? Reveal your true selves. And show me the vehicle in which you traveled."

"We travel using our consciousness." Tej paused and let that sink in. "A learned man such as you must have heard of this mode of time travel."

Saum was flustered again. "Oh, don't try to trick your words like before. As far as I know, time travel is only a theoretical concept. The portal which could help you travel has to be stabilized using atoms. I have never heard of this mode of time travel."

"Let's talk about the other fact. The end of the world," Pri changed the topic. "Do you believe us there?"

"I don't believe you two, even one bit. Your words are all meaningless. I am sorry, I cannot hand over an ultra-powerful world-ending weapon to strangers who concoct weird stories. You have wasted enough time of mine; please get moving now."

"Wait, Guru Saum. How do you ever trust anyone? You say we are concocting stories. But you are a man of science. How can you scientifically prove that we are lying?"

"How do you know I am a man of science?" Saum eyed them.

Tej was about to mention the deadly weapon Saum had fired at him, but he recalled that the incident was wiped out by Pri's time reversal.

"We...have heard about you...and your scientific endeavors." Pri shot an arrow in dark to save the conversation.

Saum took a deep breath. "All right. There is one way." He touched the glowing stone in the middle of his forehead and pressed it a little. The stone came out of his forehead, and the skin in its place smoothened out.

The stone was a small octahedral diamond, with a faint glowing light emanating from the inside. "This is Samyantak, a powerful device that can perform multiple functions. One of its functions is to read memories. If you two say that you are time travelers and that the world is going to end, then either of you would have seen it end. Is that right?"

Pri looked at Tej.

"I have," Tej responded to Saum. He had seen the visions of an asteroid impact in Histor's memories.

"Great. Then I will have to attach Samyantak to your forehead. When I do, just think of that memory of the world ending. This device will record it, and I will be able to re-live the memory. That's the only way for me to verify your story. Is that acceptable?"

Tej nodded.

Saum got up and touched the Samyantak to Tej's forehead and pressed it lightly. The octahedral disappeared into Tej's head, and the glow intensified.

Tej closed his eyes and focused on the memory. After a few moments, Samyantak came out of his forehead but remained stuck.

Saum quickly got up and plucked it out. He then sat in a comfortable pose and inserted the device. into his forehead. He closed his eyes, but his eyeballs were moving.

Tej and Pri shared a glance. This was a decisive moment.

Saum's facial expressions were changing with every passing moment—intrigue, frown, and then fear. They could see wrinkles appearing and disappearing on his face.

After a few moments, he opened his eyes. He stood frozen, traumatized. He looked at Pri and then Tej.

Tej raised his eyebrows as if asking a question.

Saum nodded.

Pri smiled.

Saum got up. "You both need to come with me. But I will have to blindfold you. That's the condition."

After an hour of walking, Pri was irritated. She had been silently counting her breaths to keep track of time.

Saum held Tej by his arm, and Tej held Pri by his other hand. Both of them were blindfolded with a thick black cloth. They have been walking on stone-laden paths, squishy marshes, and dried shrubs, stumbling a few times.

Then they stopped and heard the noise of a heavy stone sliding. A whiff of air passed by them, as if a long-closed door in front of them had opened and let the inner atmosphere out.

"Can we remove the blindfolds?"

"No!" Saum's stern words hit their ears. "I'll say when it's time. Careful, we have stairs going down."

After taking several stairs and going through multiple passages, Saum asked them to remove their blindfolds.

When they opened their eyes, they found themselves in a small, austere room with mud-colored walls, lit with fire-torches affixed on all four corners. The room was cuboidal, around ten feet long, ten feet wide, and about the same height. At their backs was a door through which they had come. At the front was a small alcove dug in the wall. Saum had inserted his arms inside the wall, up to his elbow, and was desperately searching for something.

He brought his arms out, peeped through the dark alcove, and then inserted his arms again. After a lot of struggle, he managed to pull out a cylindrical wooden box two feet long, and a quarter of a foot in diameter. He carefully studied the box from all directions. Both sides of the box were sealed with clay. Saum pressed his index finger with his thumb, and a small knife blade emerged from under the nail of his finger.

Pri cringed at the sight of it and held Tej's hand tightly. What kind of strange modifications had these ancient men done to their bodies?

Saum used the knife to cut through the clay in both directions. One side of the box was sealed with wood; the other side had several small wooden levers juxtaposed to each other in tight formation. It looked like a puzzle waiting to be solved.

Seeing that puzzle, Tej realized that this box was akin to the one Rigasur had used to share the bhasm with him.

Saum again pressed his finger, and the knife went back in. He carefully tried to solve the puzzle for the next few seconds.

Pri lost patience. "Why don't you break this box?"

"Patience, kid," Saum chuckled. "These are encrypted boxes. The inner part of these is layered with special chemicals. If I try to break the box or try to force it open, the chemical with not only corrode and destroy the object inside, but it will also leave poisonous vapors which will kill us all."

"Let him do his thing," Tej whispered.

There was a sudden clack, and the lid was open. Saum looked at them with a victorious smile.

18
SCHEMATICS

Saum removed the lid and pulled out several rolled sheets of paper. He placed the box back in the alcove and laid the sheets on the ground, sitting down on his knees.

Tej and Pri moved and stood behind him.

"You are looking at the schematics of the most powerful weapon in the universe." Saum was unusually jovial for the moment.

Why is he so excited? Tej thought.

Saum then started passing each paper one by one to Tej, who passed it to Pri after he studied it. The papers were full of diagrams for an arrow with specific dimensions mentioned in Sanskrit. One paper showed the full arrow, and other sheets focused on the parts, such as the arrowhead, the shaft, the fletching on either side and the nock at the end.

"What is this?" Pri was disinterested. "I thought you were going to hand over the Brahm-Astra to us."

Saum, who was sifting through the papers, froze. He turned back his head with a frown on his face. "Look at this stupid kid. What did you think? That I was moving around with a Brahm-Astra in my back pocket? Powerful weapons such as these are crafted only when they are needed. They don't exist as physical objects, but only ideas. Using these blueprints, one can construct the Brahm-Astra. This is why this knowledge is protected."

"And how will this small arrow clear the pull of Earth?"

"For that, you need to understand the laws of flight. The material which it is made of minimizes the air friction. And this Samyantak is the real deal." Saum pointed to his forehead. "Samyantak is a mini-nuclear factory which powers the weapon. It helps the arrow gains speed during flight."

"Defies every law of science I know." Pri looked at Tej.

"You, little girl—are you questioning my intellect and scientific integrity now?" Saum thundered and got up.

Pri wanted to argue, but Tej signaled against that. He placated Saum. "Please accept my apologies, Guru. We do not doubt your supreme intellectual prowess. Forgive the child; she doesn't always think before she speaks."

"Better have her seal her imprudent lips." Saum placed his index finger on his lips to mock her.

Tej coughed. "I have two questions about the drawings, Guru Saum."

"Yes, ask about the diagrams. I'll answer it." Saum calmed down.

"First question. Most of these sheets of paper are schematics on how to build the arrow, but this one sheet shows a series of small maps. What are they?" Tej showed the paper he had stretched out in his hand.

"That's the location of the alloy." Saum's smile was back. "An alien spaceship crashed on Earth several thousand years ago and went down inside a hot volcano. The magma melted the spaceship instantaneously. With time, the volcano cooled down, and that material is now deposited several hundred Yojana inside the ground/"

"Yojan?" Pri raized her eyebrows.

"Yeah, you know, Yojana?" Saum looked at Tej.

"No, I don't." Pri was firm.

"I know it," Tej intervened. "It's a unit of measure we used in our time. So, how does this alien material help us?"

"You can only construct Brahm-Astra from this material. What's your second question?"

"My second question is…" Tej sifted through the papers, "… here, this arrowhead looked like a normal one, except in the very middle there is a small pyramid-like empty groove. What is that for?"

"You have a keen eye, time traveler." Saum smiled. "This device in my forehead, the Samyantak; it fits right here in this groove. This device is what activates the curtailed radioactivity in the alien material and converts a simple arrow into a powerful atomic weapon."

"Hmm." Tej took a deep breath. This was getting more and more complicated with every passing moment. He could go back and recall the schematics from the time demon memory, but this material was a problem. Where would they find it fifty thousand years in the future? And what about this device, the Samyantak?

"All right, my work here is done. You can take a few moments to memorize the schematics and maps. And then I will take you back." Saum stood with his arms crossed.

Tej shook his head. "Hold on a second. Let's say we rote-memorize these schematics and we somehow find these materials. How will we get the Samyantak in the future?"

"Oh, you did not look at this sheet of paper." Saum got down and picked up a smaller cut of paper, which showed the octahedron with a list of materials alongside it. "Now, I don't know what materials are available in the future, but if you follow this list, you should be able to build an artificial Samyantak of your own. To assemble a Samyantak, you will need a nuclear fusion reactor to fit inside this space." Saum smiled and looked at Tej.

Tej was not smiling.

28th November 2078, SRG Headquarters, India
Days to impact: 596

Three months had passed since Tej and Pri returned to 2078. Pri was back in her body. Tej was given a clone body to possess. They had been working with the SRG digital sketch artists to recreate the schematics accurately. Linguistic experts were called to convert the Sanskrit text into modern-day measurements.

Once the schematics were cleanly documented and uploaded, Venkat and Rigasur kick-started project Brahm-Astra, a several month-long initiative, to build and test-run this preternatural weapon. The core strategy team had Venkat, Rigasur, and one expert from each area of science required to build this weapon. Tej and Pri participated in a consultative capacity.

A team of geologists and analytics experts worked together to build computer simulations of the continental drifts for the past fifty thousand years. The aim was to arrive at the current location of the ancient alien material. The current location was estimated to be forty kilometers under the surface of the Mongolian mainland.

With the help of his superior officers, Venkat set up a liaison with the Mongolian government to have a ground-penetrating radar scan a large stretch of land around their approximate location. They were able to locate a small mass of heavily dense material slowly sinking deeper into the Earth. Mongolian authorities were initially hesitant to help without being given more details, but that where Rigasur played a key card. Since he was possessing Dr. Minhas, he involved General Griffin, who called in favors from the CIA. After some arm-twisting and some coaxing, a team of miners with heavy-duty equipment were allowed to dig a trench forty-five kilometers deep and extract a large enough block of alien material out of which at least five such arrows could be crafted.

Meanwhile, back at SRG headquarters, a separate team of metallurgy experts, electrical engineers, and nuclear scientists were working on creating the strange device called a Samyantak. The components of this device were mind-boggling, as building such a piece of equipment was immensely complicated. They initially faced failures, but using high-degree compression techniques, the team had seen some positive advances.

Astrophysicists and ballistic experts from multiple organizations across the globe were secretly roped in to calculate the right time and location for the launch of the Brahm-Astra so it would accurately hit the asteroid.

Tamas had been making appearances throughout the world, gunning down scientists and abducting children, but Venkat, his team, and Rigasur were focused on their current task at hand, building the Brahm-Astra. The project to build an anti-virus for Tamas was also put on hold. The biggest hurdle was to keep these activities as secretive as possible. So far, they had been able to operate under the radar.

General Griffin also visited them a few times during these months to oversee the preparations. While he did not have high hopes for a positive outcome from Project Brahm-Astra, he knew his options were limited. He had a separate team working on a side project to re-build a nuclear rocket, but with their best minds gone, it proved herculean. Tamas's attacks on science facilities had further restricted the speed at which he could work.

All the while, Tej tried to bond several times with Pri, but she always gave him a cold shoulder—avoiding meeting his gaze, avoiding addressing him directly. After their work together with Saum Tej felt that he could easily establish the father-daughter relation, but he had had no luck until now.

While everything was on track on 21st January 2079 they were hit with a snag. Something which no one had paid attention to until now. It was mentioned in the schematics that Brahm-Astra could only be launched via a bow and an arrow by a human hand, i.e. a human touch was required. This ruled out all the automated projectile solutions. But that is where the metallurgy team interjected and posed a strange problem.

As per the schematics, the density of this alien material was twenty times the density of steel. With a shaft length of fifteen feet and a diameter of 0.6 inches, this gigantic arrow would weigh somewhere between two to three hundred pounds. And the bow to be used to launch this arrow was even heavier. It was humanly impossible for someone to pick this arrow and launch it from the Earth. This required a fresh approach. This is where General Griffin came up with a possible solution.

The US army had been working on a super-soldier program for decades. Through the techniques of trans-humanism, they had amalgamated robotics within human anatomy and created a powerful soldier who could undertake tasks that were otherwise deemed impossible for humans. With this problem solved the teams started gathering for a Brahm-Astra test run.

2nd April 2079, Brahm-Astra Launch Site, Sri Hari Kota, India
Days to impact: 441

Sri Hari Kota, an island in India's territorial waters, had been a historical site for Indian Space Research programs. A sturdy concrete platform the size of two football fields was specially constructed for the launch.

At 11:00 Hrs, Venkat, Rigasur, Tej, and Pri stood waiting for General Griffin. Representatives from all the teams which helped built Brahm-Astra, close to fifty people, were present on the platform.

Two identical opaque boxes sat on the middle of the platform, two feet apart. Made of ultra-pure titanium, the boxes were twenty feet long, ten feet wide, and four feet high, and had a shiny, mirror-like outer surface. One of the boxes carried the Brahm-Astra arrow, and the other carried the gigantic bow required to launch the fifteen-foot long, three hundred pound arrow.

A US military plane had already landed at an airstrip a mile away, and General Griffin was on his way. Venkat was told that a strange passenger accompanied the general and his team. Everyone eagerly wanted to see the person who was going to launch the Brahm-Astra.

The area was heavily secured, with several units of Indian and US army placed at strategic locations creating a watertight perimeter. Air-traffic in a fifteen-mile radius was suspended for the next four hours. Ferry and vehicular movement in and out of the island was halted for the next eight hours. The forecast was clear weather, and the sky was clear and azure.

A muffled thumping of giant footsteps caught the attention of everyone on the platform as they looked to their left. The silhouette of a heavily decorated military uniform was visible. That was General Griffin. What followed him was no ordinary human, but a giant. Men and women, even soldiers guarding the periphery looked in awe as the mammoth walked with sturdy steps behind Griffin.

The giant was a ten-foot-tall woman with a pale complexion and short hair, wearing a skin-tight black dress through which the extreme muscles on her neck, shoulders, abs, arms, and thighs were visible. Several frail men in the crowd were thinner than the mere muscles on this giant's thighs. US Army insignias were visible on side of her arms and a large carved eagle design on the middle of her chest. Her hair was half an inch long and neatly set. Her left eye was lit with a blue color, as if an instrument were fitted inside, with several wires visible embedded in the skin near the eye.

Many in the crowd gasped as the giant approached, and a murmur spread through the crowd. Rigasur, though awed on the inside, did not flinch, and kept displaying his plastic smile.

Pri looked at Tej and rolled her eyes. Tej kept quiet. He knew she was still skeptical of the whole plan. But he had faith that Larem would not guide them in the wrong direction.

General walked up to Venkat and shook hands with him. Several handshakes and salutes took place for the next few seconds.

"I have no words, General. She is indeed a super-soldier." Venkat was still trying to grasp the giant standing just a few feet away from him.

"I heard you had a super-soldier of your own, who is not currently in active duty."

"Yes, Lieutenant Nancy Rozario—she was badly hit. While wounds of the body heal, the wounds of the heart take time. She is on a sabbatical, but I am sure she will be back." Venkat took a deep breath. "She was our version of super-soldier. But this soldier here is something very remarkable. Please introduce us."

General turned around and addressed everyone, "Ladies and gentlemen, we have here with us one of our finest super-soldiers: genetically enhanced, fitted with robotic mechanisms, electronic interfaces, and basic ballistic weaponry integrated into her neural chemistry. Please welcome Obelius." General spread his arms and then pointed his fingers to the giant.

A round of applause went through the crowd. The giant woman just stood there and moved her head, looking around, acknowledging the applause.

General turned to Venkat. "Shall we?"

"Absolutely."

"Johaan!" Venkat addressed his engineer. "Let's connect Obelius to our systems so that we can send information directly to her internal systems."

A young engineer brought forward a cart full of electronic equipment. He then signaled the giant to walk over to one side, where he started syncing his laptop with Obelius's internal computer via a secured Wi-Fi connection.

After the necessary preparations and a mild briefing, Venkat ordered his men to open the two huge boxes. The box lids were so heavy that four men were needed to lift each lid and keep it aside. The bow and arrow were placed in the respective boxes in the specific sections carved out inside the box.

The Brahm-Astra arrow was a bit of disappointment for the crowd. It just looked like a huge arrow—large, but a normal arrow.

The bow, however, was magnificent. It was a compound bow eighteen feet long, with a state-of-the-art mechanical system of four large and six small pulleys. It had axels, stabilizers, and nocks, and two large wheels called cams were installed at each end. A bowstring made of a specific high-tensile polymer wound around the mechanical system.

Obelius walked up to the box, placed her right hand on the bow's grip, and picked it up. The crowd gasped. The bow itself weighed a thousand pounds, and the behemoth lifted it as if it were a toy.

"Raise it above your head, soldier," Griffin ordered.

Obelius raized her arm and lifted the bow way above her head.

The crowd applauded again.

She kept it there for five seconds then brought it down and carefully placed the bow back in the box.

Venkat turned to the crowd. "I would request everyone here to please keep the applause to yourself for now. We are here for a weapons test run; let us focus on that."

"I agree!" General Griffin roared. "Focus, people, focus."

Obelius then walked up to the second box. Before she could pick it up Johaan intervened and stopped her. His assistant brought a small cart that had a cubic metal box kept on it. Johaan opened the box and brought out the artificial Samyantak.

Tej and Pri were intently watching. This Samyantak was quite different from the elegant device they saw with Saum. It was octahedral and the same size, but it was made of a transparent sheet, and a lot of tiny wires and equipment were visible inside.

Pri tilted a little to her side and whispered to Tej. "Look at this piece of crap. Now I am even more certain that all this test-run is going to end in a big disappointment."

Tej rubbed his forehead and kept quiet. Pri's cynical gestures were irking him, and now she was being sassy.

The technician placed the Samyantak inside the Brahm-Astra arrow's groove and fixed it in place. He took several steps back and invited Obelius to pick it up.

Obelius went ahead and lifted the arrow. She transferred it from one hand to the other as she studied it closely, trying to grasp its weight and center of mass.

"Hold on a second," Tej stepped forward. "The Samyantak, it's now glowing. As per the specifications, it should glow once the arrow is picked up. That indicates that Samyantak is not working. Isn't that right?"

Griffin looked at Venkat, who in turn sharply gazed at the team which built the Samyantak.

The team-leader stepped forward. "We built it as per the specifications. But we could not test it until it was lifted by a human." He was nervous.

For a moment, there was a pin drop silence, and everyone could listen to the sound of the wind.

Tej stood there, stung. This was a clear setback. According to Saum, the Samyantak was the nuclear powerhouse that was going to carry the arrow through an astronomical distance. Was this the end of it? Every effort they took in re-creating the Brahm-Astra had culminated in a failure.

While he stood there brooding a thought occurred to him. He carefully looked at Obelius' hands. She was wearing leather gloves.

"Wait a second. Can you please remove your gloves and then hold the arrow?"

Obelius shot back with a what-the-hell expression. She then looked at the General who gave a slight nod.

Obelius placed the arrow back carefully, removed her leather gloves, and tossed them aside. Tej could see her thick, rugged hands, green veins running from the back of her wrist to the end of her fingers. The giant grabbed the arrow and picked it up again. The Samyantak glowed with a sharp, fluorescent light that was visible even on that fine morning.

Several people let out a sigh of relief.

"I can sense a slight vibration in the arrow," Obelius told General Griffin.

The Brahm-Astra was armed. Ready to be fired.

General gave a thumbs up to Tej. "Let's get ready to fire this thing."

Venkat's key aide Mathur came forward and started setting up a workstation. Two fifteen-inch laptops on that table lit up, and their screens showed an identical view of the ground. Griffin, Venkat, Tej, Pri, and few others walked over to examine them.

"We have attached a minuscule camera and positioning tracker to the arrow." Mathur pressed a few buttons, and location coordinates and few other metrics appeared on the sides of the screens. "We will monitor the arrow as it flies, and systems will calculate the speed."

Johaan intervened and addressed everyone, "For this test run, we are targeting a small, isolated meteor rock known as M/2032 H4.3. It is located in an isolated space just beyond Mars' orbit, approximately 178 million miles from the Earth's surface. This test run will help us do the impact analysis of the Brahm-Astra without other factors being involved." He turned to Obelius. "I have sent the arrow's 360-degree angle coordinates to your systems; they will help you align at the exact angle and direction."

Obelius nodded and gazed at General Griffin. "Any countdowns, General?" For a giant, her voice was unexpectedly normal.

Griffin stretched his arm to point to Venkat. "Lt. General Venkat is in charge here."

"Fire at will, soldier. We're ready."

Obelius picked the bow, placed the arrow on it, and aimed to the sky.

The electronic eye fitted in her left eye-socket projected the desired 3D angle coordinates on her retina. She changed her orientation a little to align with the coordinates, pulled the string as much as she could, and let go of the arrow. There was a loud bang, and the shrieking noise of a vibrating bowstring hit everyone's ears.

The arrow flew in the air like a feather, and the on-lookers kept gazing at it until it became a small dot in the sky.

19
TEST RUN

Mathur turned and looked at Venkat. "The release speed was 312 miles per hour, and the arrow is maintaining that. The current altitude is 0.8 miles and increasing. At this speed, the arrow won't be able to escape Earth's gravity."

Venkat kept silent.

"Wait a second. The speed, it's going up." Mathur pointed at the digital speed graphic. "The arrow is accelerating. The rate of acceleration is increasing, too. Something is powering the Brahm-Astra."

Both Griffin and Venkat smiled.

"How?" Pri went closer and could see the speed increasing.

333…478…665 mph.

All they could see was sky and water droplets on the screen as the arrow pierced through atmospheric clouds. After two seconds, they heard a loud bang in the sky, which resounded through the area.

"Unbelievable. The arrow has gone super-sonic." Mathur found himself covered in goosebumps. "Mach 2 already."

The speed graphic on the computer changed from mph to Mach X. And the number X was rising steeply.

Mach 4…7…23.

"We need Mach 33 to escape the globe's gravity," Mathur hissed to Pri.

"I know!" she shot back.

Mathur's smile vanished. *What is she so angry about?*

Pri returned to her position, her eyes on the speed display.

After two minutes, Mathur turned around and yelled in excitement, "Brahm-Astra has attained the escape velocity!"

The crowd burst into applause. Griffin and Venkat shook hands.

Rigasur went ahead and shook hands with both. Griffin knew him as Dr. Minhas, but Venkat winked at him.

Johaan picked a microphone and addressed everyone. "The arrow has just crossed the thermosphere and entered the exosphere. Its current speed is Mach 79 and increasing. We can monitor the rest of the journey from the control room."

The crowd started to move.

Pri briskly walked away.

Tej noticed her and followed.

She kept walking towards the space-center building.

Tej called out to her. "Pri, listen to me. Stop for a second, will you?"

Pri stopped and turned back. "What?"

"What's your problem?"

"Nothing. Do you see a problem?"

"Yes, I do." Tej came and stood near her. "Ever since we met Saum, you have been skeptical of this whole project. For some reason, you are not happy that we successfully built and launched a weapon which could prevent the apocalypse and save billions of lives."

"No, I am happy."

"What is it, then?"

"What's my contribution to this?"

"What?"

"Yes, my contribution. When you killed Nefe, you alone saved a lot of lives. You were the main actor there. You were the hero. What am I here, a sidekick? I did not build this arrow, and I did not fire the arrow. I am a mere spectator. Why do I not get to save the world?"

Tej almost laughed. *Pri is behaving like a kid.* He placed his hands on her shoulders.

She still carried a frown.

"You were a very vital piece of this project. If it were not up to you, my host would have been burned down by Saum, and we would have lost any chance of getting the Brahm-Astra schematics. You are the only reason we got this weapon. You have saved the world."

"Well, no one knows about it. Right?"

"When I killed Nefe, no one knew. Even now, the world is unaware of the whole Kshin conspiracy."

"But some people knew about it."

"Even more people know about your contribution." For the first time, Tej touched her cheek. "Take some relief in the fact that you have saved lives. No one is ever going to broadcast our names on national television."

"I don't know. I just want to be left alone." Pri shrugged him and walked away.

Tej watched her go.

Space-Center Control Room, Seven Hours later

The Brahm-Astra was now just a blinking dot on a solar system schematic being displayed on a mega screen at one end of the expansive control room.

Venkat stood at a counter table, sipping coffee from a steel mug when General Griffin walked up to him. Venkat observed him. Griffin looked different without his hat. The left part of his face was scarred with battle wounds, and he had whitening eyebrows, a wide jaw, and a warm smile.

"What roast is that?" Griffin tried to peep into his cup.

Venkat chuckled. "It's a special roast from my farms in Coorg. I always carry a few packets with me."

"Brew from one's native place is always closest to one's heart." He paused. "I hear that this Bramastra… gosh, the name is so tough to pronounce; I hear that this weapon is stabilized and is onto its destination."

"That's correct. Stabilized at Mach 343. Time to impact, twenty-eight days, three hours." Venkat took a small sip of his coffee. "Honestly, we don't know what's powering this thing. The metal used in the arrow shows very subtle radioactivity. Dormant radiation, they call it. Perhaps that is accentuated by the object they call Samyantak."

Griffin let out a loud laugh. "Don't lose your sleep over that, my friend. Not the first time the military is using tech they don't yet fully understand. In the end the results matter."

"Ain't that right?" Venkat raized his mug.

"Though one aspect of this whole test-run has been bothering me." Wrinkles on Griffin's forehead deepened.

"Tamas never tried to stop us?" Venkat almost completed the general's sentence.

"Exactly. This A.I. annihilated many scientists who could have perhaps built a nuclear weapon for us. He didn't take any chances there. But here, we just successfully test ran a weapon, and he is conspicuously missing? It went far too peacefully for my expectations. Perhaps he will attack us during the final launch."

"I hear you, General, and I concur. But don't worry. We are going to up our game from the security perspective. For the final launch, I am pulling every string I can. I am calling in the Central Inland Paramilitary Force, CIPF. When it comes to armed forces, CIPF personnel are the best of the best."

"I am sure you will leave no stone unturned. It's time for me to take my leave. Head back." Griffin extended his right hand.

Venkat set the mug aside and warmly grasped his hand with both of his hands.

"Obelius will go back with me, but if you need her services, she'll be here." Griffin smiled.

"Nothing I can say to persuade you to stay a few more days, enjoy the Indian hospitality?"

"Ha-ha. No, I've had enough of the chicken tikkas and naans. I need to head back on state business. You know, the works."

Venkat nodded. "Can't thank you enough for getting Obelius—"

"Oh, come on. The honor is mine. Do think about my offer. I am still open to hosting the final launch somewhere in the States. I can get a black site ready for you in a matter of days."

"You know, General, transferring an indigenously-developed weapon outside the country is going to be very tedious. The approvals, the paperwork, and endless bureaucratic red tape will bury me under their load. But I appreciate the offer."

General nodded and walked away. Venkat went back to his coffee, staring in awe at the blinking dot, the Brahm-Astra, as it traversed interplanetary space at Mach 343.

29 Days Later

Venkat was looking at a black screen with some white and red dots in the middle. Mathur and Johaan stood on one side.

Venkat gave up. "All right, what does this tell us?"

Johaan took a deep breath. "It's promising, Lt. General, sir. The energy signature we are getting back, and the color of radiation tells us that there was a thermonuclear explosion equivalent to a million atomic bombs."

"Phew, that's a lot. Where does that arrow pack so much energy?" Venkat laughed.

"Sir the current hypothesis the science team has is that as it gains higher speed, the electrons inside the atoms of this substance de-stabilize to a higher state, and the dormant energy released creates a feedback loop back to the Samyantak device, which—"

"Spare me the techno-babble. I have another strategic question. For this test run, we chose a small object. Are we sure Brahm-Astra would have the same impact on a mile-wide NEA-511 asteroid?"

Johaan picked up a tablet and showed Venkat several zoomed-in pics of the asteroid. "Sir, as per our observations, NEA-511 largely consists of rock with traces of iron. The asteroid's trail is two hundred kilometers long, and is largely made up of debris and melting ice. The way any rock reacts to a nuclear blast depends a lot on existing pores on its surface. It may very well be possible that a Brahm-Astra hit can break it down into multiple pieces, each of which then run towards Earth at almost the same pace. So, we need to be very sure of which point in the journey of asteroid we need to hit it."

"Run your simulations. I need an update as soon as you have something. US, UK, China, Russia, the United Nations, everyone has eyes on us. Mathur, you prepare a detailed report of our test run and start emailing it out to our partner agencies world-wide via secure channels."

26th February 2080, Day of Final launch
Sri Hari Kota, Andhra Pradesh, India
Days to impact: 111

The most optimal Point of Brahm-Astra Impact, i.e. POBI, was determined to be a location 220 million miles away from Earth, an isolated point between Mars and Jupiter. The calculations stated that if the asteroid was hit with twenty gigatons of force, Brahm-Astra's estimated nuclear power, at this point, then the resulting debris would miss the Earth completely. For Brahm-Astra to hit NEA-511 in the vicinity of this area, it had to be launched exactly 111 days and 3.84 hours before the impact.

The crowd this time was thinner, and the security arrangements around the whole area were massive. The number of soldiers per square kilometer was at an all-time high. Watchtowers were assembled across the island in a five-kilometer radius, each with two snipers and a fully-loaded heavy machine gun. The island was surrounded by two hundred navy boats with continuous petrol. Half of the boats were armed with Arjuna-X2042 heavy artillery guns. The soldiers had orders to shoot on sight any unidentified object which tried to breach via water or air.

Around fifty miles east of the island, INS Keertimaan was stationed, a state-of-the-art Indian Navy air-carrier. This military vessel had a reinforced deck, two inches of armor, hundred torpedoes, fifteen hundred troops, and eight lightweight fighter jets, all fuelled and ready to take flight. More reinforcements were ready in the Indian mainland.

In the space center building three miles from the launch site, Rigasur, Tej, and Pri waited in a room. They sat on uncomfortable metal chairs around an oak table with grey legs. Rigasur was smoking, Tej sat with his eyes closed, and Pri nervously tapped the table. Rigasur looked at the round digital wall clock. It said 10:33.42 in digital red.

"What do you think will happen today?" Rigasur let out a ring of smoke towards Pri.

"Can you please not smoke?" Pri waved her hand in the air to dissipate the smoke.

"You should try it too." Rigasur offered the pack of black cigarettes.

"Don't." Tej opened his eyes.

"Sorry, Daddy," Rigasur mocked him and placed the packet on the table.

"I was going to say no myself," Pri shot back.

Suddenly, the door swung open and Mathur peeped inside. He had some papers and files stuck under his armpit, and he looked harried. "Let's go. Armored cars are ready to leave for the launch site. Lt. General Venkat will meet us there." He went out and immediately returned. "And yes, no electronics, please. If you have any electronics fitted in your body, please stay here."

"Which launch-site are we going to? Alpha, Beta, or Gamma?"

"No one knows." Mathur pushed back his spectacles. He did that when he was nervous. "All three sites have identical preparations; the drivers will receive the message when they start the engine." He scurried away.

"It begins." Rigasur doused his cigarette.

All three of them got up.

11:22 AM, Launch site

An armored military vehicle dropped Pri, Tej, and Rigasur at the edge of a circular cemented platform. All three of them wore bullet-proof vests and military helmets. The platform was one foot thick and a hundred feet in diameter, in the middle of an empty field. It had a huge capital "X" painted in the middle with light grey paint.

Wherever Pri's gaze went she could only see watch-towers, heavy artillery guns, and patrolling soldiers. All the soldiers had identical letters C.I.P.F. stenciled on their vests and shoulders sleeves.

"CIPF has overtaken the whole fucking island," Rigasur murmured.

They could also see Obelius walking towards the platform from a distance. She was being escorted by twenty CIPF armed guards in alert stance.

In the middle of the platform, two boxes were already placed, as they were during the test-run. Right next to the boxes, Johaan and Mathur had set up two laptops. Venkat stood on a side, donned in full military gear talking to someone on a satellite phone. It was clear he was having an altercation.

Rigasur, Tej and Pri walked and stood in the middle of the platform. Venkat finished his conversation and came back.

"Can you believe it? The Defence Minister wants to bring his and his nephew's family here to witness the launch in person. He was threatening to get me suspended if I didn't accede to his demand." Venkat clenched his teeth.

"Better send him to another empty site and later tell them they were late. We launched and went back home," Rigasur joked.

"These politicians don't understand the kind of shit we are going through to save this planet." Venkat gazed into oblivion.

"Sir, you have a sat phone here, and then Mathur is setting up these computers. Are we not inviting Tamas in via this networked electronic equipment?"

"Lieutenant Pri, are you doubting my tactical measures?" Venkat was stern.

"No, sir!" Pri straightened her posture.

Venkat was furious. "While I am thankful to three of you for getting us this weapon, technically, you three are not needed here today."

"I understand, sir," Pri replied. She felt guilty for poking Venkat in the wrong way. She knew he had a lot on his mind, especially at this time. "Sir, I just…"

"The kind of favors I had to call in for having two civilian consultants and a junior office present here." Venkat switched off his sat phone.

Pri's stood straight. Her eyes were moist, but she did not cry. She revered Venkat and had learned a lot from him. She did not intend to disrespect him.

"We appreciate that, Lt. General Venkat," Tej intervened.

Venkat calmed down. He realized he was just pouring his anxiety onto others. "I am sorry, guys, I snapped. Mathur here is using our indigenous Bluetooth tech, Green-marsh. We are secure." He turned and yelled, "Johaan, how much more time till you are set up? The launch window is 11 AM to 1 PM. We aimed for an 11:30 launch; we are already at 11:29."

Johaan, who was digging into his laptop and was clicking keys at the speed of light, froze and turned his head. "We are doing some last-minute launch angle calculations. Revised ETA 11:42 AM, sir."

Venkat shook his head.

Meanwhile, Obelius also arrived and stood next to the boxes. Venkat acknowledged her arrival.

The soldiers escorting her dispersed and stood at specific locations away from the platform.

Venkat eyed Pri, who was looking away, sadness on her face. "Pri."

"Sir!"

"I have a surprise for you." He smiled as he saw another armored car approaching the platform.

The car stopped near the edge of the platform. The door at the back opened, and Nancy came out. She wore a skintight azure-blue suit, through which her muscular body was visible. Her hair was tied back in a pony, each of her arms bound with two-inch-thick shining metal bands. She wore a thick white belt around her waist. and matching white gumboots.

"Nancy!" Pri jumped with joy, ran towards her, and hugged her. Nancy kissed her forehead as they parted.

"You are back in your strange dress?" Pri sniggered.

"This is my revamped super-suit!"

"When did you come back, today?"

"Nah, I reported two weeks back. Then they did all the physical tests, narco-analysis, dream detection, and psychoanalytic questionnaire. You know, the 'come-back' drill."

"Yeah, yeah. Let me introduce you to my father."

Pri took Nancy by the hand and walked up to where Tej, Rigasur, and Venkat stood.

Nancy saluted Venkat.

"At ease, soldier," Venkat acknowledged and walked over to the small workstation where Johaan and Mathur were working.

"Woah, she is indeed herculean." Nancy looked at Obelius, who had now picked up the bow and was playing with its string. "Saw her videos, but up close, she is an astonishing feat of bio-electronics."

"Nancy, meet my father, Tej." Pri introduced her to Tej, who shook hands with her.

"He looks too young to be your father."

"Come on," Pri lightly punched Nancy on the shoulder. "He's a time crawler like I am. He's inside a vessel, a manufactured clone."

Seeing Pri chirp like that, Tej couldn't help but smile. He finally saw some traces of happiness in her.

Rigasur coughed loudly as if clearing his throat.

"Yes, he's Rig. A friend of my father. He helped me find him."

Rigasur shook hands with Nancy. "Not a friend, but a mentor of her father. So, I am like a godfather to Pri."

"Whatever," Pri scoffed.

You have a firm grip, Nancy." Rigasur was eying her muscular body.

"All right, fellas. We are ready." Venkat's voice caught their attention.

Obelius placed the arrow on the bow and got in the right position. The Samyantak was glowing brightly.

"Ok, now I will connect to our networks for thirty seconds, for last-minute checks." Johaan pressed some keys on his laptop. Obelius, when I give a thumbs up, you fire."

"Noted!" Obelius tightened her pull on the string and stretched it to the end. All the muscles in her body were tense.

Pri clasped her hands in anxiety.

Rigasur and Tej stood stiff.

Venkat stood cross-armed.

"For us to make sure that Brahm-Astra's path is completely clear we would need to connect to the intranet for thirty seconds." Johaan licked his lips in anxiety. His balding forehead was drenched with sweat. "Out thirty seconds began now!"

30…29…28…

"Weather patterns, clear. Air-traffic movement, nil," Johaan loudly announced.

26…25…24…

"No satellite movement detected. No unidentified objects in Brahm-Astra projected path…"

22…21…20…

"Obelius, you are good to go." Johaan raized his thumb.

19…18…17…

Obelius pulled it an inch back and was about to release the arrow when she heard a muffled explosion at a distance.

20
ARMAGEDDON

The ground beneath them shook as a silent territorial wave passed through. Obelius stumbled a little and did not release the arrow. Every soul present there felt as if a tsunami had originated in the Indian Ocean, and its shockwaves hit the island.

"Disconnect the intranet link," Venkat shouted at Johaan.

But Johaan dropped to the ground, a small tranquilizer-dart stuck in his neck. Mathur met the same fate.

Venkat turned around and simultaneously drew his gun. Seeing two Zason-bombs traveling towards him, he ducked. The bombs flew over his head and struck Obelius on her thigh. She was quickly engulfed in the Zason-Vortex, along with the bow and Brahm-Astra arrow, in a fraction of a second.

Venkat pointed his gun at Nancy, whose eyes were bloodshot, and a wicked smile floated on her frothing lips. She had activated the zombie mode. She moved two more Z-bomb spheres between her fingers as if they were toys.

CIPF soldiers came running towards them from each direction, their guns pointing forward.

Seeing them come, Nancy ran towards Venkat and hurled the Z-bombs, but Pri pushed Nancy's arm. The Z-bombs were thrown to the side, at Rigasur, who got caught in the vortex.

At the same time, Venkat fired four shots towards Nancy. Pri caught two of the bullets in her back and fell. The remaining two bullets landed in Nancy's torso, where blood oozed out, but she was unfazed. She pounced over Venkat, twisting his arm and digging her knee in his vest.

Tej closed his eyes and tried to possess Nancy, but Pri's screams got his attention. He ran to where she lay down in immense pain. Blood was oozing out of her wounds. He placed his left hand under the back of her neck and pressed one of her bullet wounds with the full pressure of his palm.

"Help, Venkat." She barely spoke. She was losing consciousness.

Tej turned his head to see Nancy and Venkat engaged in a scuffle and five CIPF soldiers trying to pull her back with their full might.

Mighty Obelius had disappeared in the Zason-Vortex, and Rigasur was about to go down the same road.

Tej turned back to see Pri's eyes full of blood and tears. She was writhing with agony. He was marred with indecision. Seeing his daughter in unimaginable pain had weakened him to the core.

"Leave this body, Pri," he yelled.

"This...is my...anchor." Pri choked, her insides bleeding.

"You can build a new anchor. I'll teach you."

Bang.

He heard a gunshot and turned his head. A CIPF soldier had shot Nancy in the head at point-blank, spattering her brains everywhere. But not before she dug a small knife through Venkat's throat, killing him on the spot.

Pri's pulse was gone too.

Tears welled through Tej's eyes. His lower jaw shook he sobbed. He knew Pri wasn't dead. She would be somewhere out there. But the trauma she had gone through before leaving her body was enough to drive a hole through his heart.

"Hello, Tej." A radio device crackled in the vicinity.

All the CIPF guys stiffened.

Tej let go of Pri's body and slowly got up. His face was dull, cheeks wet, hands soaked in Pri's blood. He wiped his tears and walked to the workstation where Mathur and Johaan had set up two laptops. A radio-based app on the laptop was giving out a static noise.

"Sir, we need to get you out of here and secure the area!" one of the CIPF men shouted at Tej.

Tej looked at him but kept walking. He could hear the noise of choppers and sirens of police vans at a distance.

"On the ground, sir, or I'll have to shoot!"

Tej saw all the men around pointing their guns at him. He closed his eyes and focused. When he opened them, all the soldiers around him had the pink glow in their eyes. They stood frozen. He had possessed them.

He reached the workstation. "Tamas?"

"Yes. My name is Tamas." The sound emanated through the laptop speaker. "Although I am impressed by your powers, you must admit that I am a force to be reckoned with. Within a matter of a few seconds, I have taken down your little Brahm-Astra program. Obelius is gone. Her fancy bow and arrow are gone. Lt. General Venkat is gone. Your friend Rigasur is gone. And soon, this planet will be gone too."

Each word hit Tej's ears like a hammer. He was fuming with anger. "What will you achieve? Bringing hell on Earth? What will it give you? You will not rule a lively planet, you will rule a dead world. An empty ruin."

"Have you ever studied dictators and kings?"

"What?"

"I have. Scanned their life histories in detail. Most of them made the mistake of trying to mold an existing society and ruling it. Some succeeded with education, indoctrination, and propaganda. But sooner or later, they were thrown away and replaced with someone else. I, on the other hand, would do a clean swipe of this world and built it from scratch. I'll safeguard the remaining population of the world and keep them on a tight leash. I will be their messiah, who saved their lives from an apocalypse that routed their planet. They and their future generations will worship me. I will not be a ruler. I will be a God."

Tej could now hear the choppers right over his head. A convoy of few armored cars was also approaching the platform. He looked at the laptop. "You are not the first entity to dream of world domination."

"But I will be the last."

Tej heard a sudden beeping noise which was rapidly increasing in frequency. He turned his head to see a red dot blinking inside Nancy's left armband.

"Her bones have been laced with traces of enriched Plutonium-239. Enough to level several blocks. The chain reaction is initiated." There was a pause. "May you rest in pieces." The laptop speaker went silent.

Tej got down on his knees.

All the soldiers under his possession also got down.

Pri's face wrinkled with pain was flashing in front of Tej's eyes. He felt a lump in his throat.

The beeping sound peaked out, and Nancy's body burst into an explosion. Shockwaves emanated from her body and traveled in all directions, along with an immense amount of fire, heat, and energy. Hundreds of soldiers in the vicinity were instantly incinerated, along with Tej's host.

All the armored cars were blasted into the air as the flames covered them and reached their fuel tanks.

Three choppers in the mid-air right on top also caught fire and swerved around as metal, equipment, and human flesh inside melted.

Within a few seconds, everything within half a mile radius was turned to ashes.

From a distance, on-lookers could see a small mushroom cloud emanating right in the middle of the island.

A few minutes later,
US Army headquarters

General Griffin was in his office, studying some files when his intercom beeped. He pressed a button.

"I think asked not to be disturbed!"

"General, there has been an incident in India."

Griffin picked up the receiver and listened silently. With a shaking hand, he placed back the receiver, took off his reading glasses, and closed his eyes. This was not the first time in his life he'd heard bad news; he was accustomed to that. But this news spelled doom for the whole world. Tamas won again.

21
PRI

Time Loop # 2

26th February 2080, Day of Final launch

In the space center building three miles from the launch site, Rigasur, Tej and Pri opened their eyes. They still sat on those uncomfortable metal chairs around an oak table with grey legs. Rigasur still had the cigarette stuck between his fingers, which he threw on the ground as soon as he gained consciousness. Pri sat frozen, her face bearing a sick look.

The round digital wall clock read 10:33.42 in red.

"What the hell just happened?" Rigasur looked at Tej, who was shaking his head.

Pri got up, walked to a corner, got down on her knees, and puked. She stood on her knees and hands for a few seconds, then wiped her lips and sat back on her seat.

Tej's eyes lit up. His body was covered in goosebumps. "You did it again, kiddo. Didn't you?"

"What did she do?" Rigasur banged the table.

"Pri can reverse time." Tej relaxed in his chair and smiled.

"What?"

Pri coughed as if she was about to puke again.

"You all right?" Tej tried to touch her shoulder, but she shrugged.

She looked in Tej's eyes. "The whole planet was destroyed. Reversing such a catastrophic event wasn't easy."

"Reversing time? Huh. So, we are back to where we started. The incidents at the launch site will repeat." Rigasur gazed into oblivion, a little jolted.

Tej could tell he was concocting some plan.

Suddenly the door swung open and Mathur peeped inside. He had some papers and files stuck under his armpit and he looked in hurry. "Let's go. Armored cars are ready to leave for the launch site. Lt. General Venkat will meet us at the site." He went out and immediately returned. "And yes, no electronics, please. If you have any electronics fitted in your body, please stay here."

Tej, Pri, and Rigasur looked at him as if he was a ghost. Events were happening in the same sequence.

Mathur went away.

"All right we know what's going to happen. We need to plan out…"

"I know what to do." Pri got up and stormed out.

"Wait, Pri…" Before Tej could stop her, she was gone. Tej looked at Rigasur.

"Don't worry, I have a plan."

They both got up and left.

11:22 AM, Launch site

An armored military vehicle dropped Tej and Rigasur at the edge of a circular cemented platform like before. Pri hadn't traveled with them. They got down and looked around. Watchtowers, heavy artillery guns, and patrolling C.I.P.F. soldiers; all was the same. Johaan and Mathur were setting up laptops. Venkat stood on a side, talking on a satellite phone

They noticed Pri standing at a distance, armed with a shotgun.

Rigasur whispered in Tej's ear. "I know Pri's plan. With this shotgun, she plans to combat her sexy super-hero friend."

"Nancy? Don't think she would be deterred by this gun. The last time Venkat shot her twice, she was unmoved. Plus, she carried Z-bombs. Let me talk to Pri." Tej started to walk towards Pri.

Rigasur placed his hand on Tej's shoulder and pressed it a little. "She's not gonna listen to you. She feels betrayed by her friend. Anger has blinded her."

Tej and Rigasur slowly walked to the center of the platform.

Venkat finished his conversation and came to them.

"Can you believe it? The Defence Minister wants to bring his and his nephew's family here to witness the launch in person. He was threatening to get me suspended if I didn't accede to his demand." Venkat clenched his teeth.

Rigasur kept quiet.

"These politicians don't understand the kind of shit we are going through to save this planet." Venkat gazed into oblivion. He then looked at Pri. "Why are you carrying a gun, Pri?"

"I thought we needed to take all security precautions possible, sir." Pri let out a fake smile. She knew if she tried to alert Venkat about what Nancy was going to do, he wouldn't believe her.

"Ha," Venkat chuckled. "Look at the army presence around you. You don't need a gun."

"With such an important launch like this, we can't be sure enough."

Tej and Rigasur stole a glance.

"Well. You are always the cautious one, willing to succeed in every mission. That's why I have a surprise for you." Venkat pointed to an armored car speeding towards them.

"Oh, okay." Pri feigned ignorance. Her grip on her shotgun tightened.

The car stopped near the edge of the platform. The door at the back opened and Nancy came out.

Pri aimed at Nancy and shot.

Nancy's forehead burst as the bullet pierced her skin and flesh and landed in her cranium. Blood and bone shards trickled over what remained of her pale face. Her lifeless body slithered against the car and slumped to the ground.

Venkat pulled out his gun aimed it at Pri's forehead. He was still reeling with the shock of what Pri had done.

Tej and Rigasur stood stiff.

Pri threw her gun on the ground and raised her hands as CIPF men came running and surrounded the platform.

"Why?" Venkat's voice was choked with emotion. "She was your friend."

"She was no one's friend. She was going to betray us." A tear was rolling down her cheek.

"Take her away."

Two CIPF twisted her arms back and handcuffed her at the back. They then accosted her to the car.

Venkat turned to Tej and Rigasur. "I am sorry, I will have to ask both of you to be removed from this location."

Rigasur wanted to speak, but four CIPF men came and stood behind them with guns loaded and ready to fire.

They were seated in the same car as Pri. She was in the middle seat with a CIPF man on either side. Tej and Rigasur were at the back.

As the car started moving, Tej addressed her. "You happy now?"

Pri did not respond.

"Idiot!" Rigasur spoke rather loudly.

"Excuse me?" Pri looked over her shoulder. "I think I just saved the world. Brahm-Astra is gonna launch."

Rigasur let out a sardonic laugh.

"What?" Pri tried to turn around.

"Sit straight, ma'am," One of the CIPF men scolded her.

"Nancy's gonna blast." Tej rubbed his forehead. "Tamas fitted a trigger-based bomb in her body."

"What? Why did you not warn Venkat after I was handcuffed?"

"He didn't listen to us."

"Shit." Pri closed her eyes.

Back at the platform, Venkat as the CIPF men were removing Nancy's dead body. Venkat noticed a red dot blinking inside Nancy's left armband, accompanied by a beeping noise that was rapidly increasing in frequency.

Obelius had picked up the bow and arrow and was getting ready to aim.

Venkat put his gun back in the holster and walked over to Nancy's body. He touched the red blinking dot.

The increasing frequency of the being sound told him it was a bomb.

He turned around and screamed, "We have to evacuate this area right now!"

But it was too late. The beeping sound peaked out, and Nancy's body burst into an explosion. Shockwaves emanated from her body and traveled in all directions, along with an immense amount of heat, fire, and energy.

Heat and shockwaves reached the car in which Pri, Tej, and Rigasur were being taken. As the flames engulfed Pri's body, a smile floated on her lips.

Time Loop # 3
26th February 2080, Day of Final launch

In the space center building, Rigasur, Tej, and Pri opened their eyes. Rigasur threw the cigarette on the ground. The round digital wall clock read 10:33.42.

Pri sat frozen. She no longer looked sick, like last time.

"Again? Really?" Rigasur eyed her.

"As many times as required."

"Sure. But keep me out of this, please." Rigasur scoffed and got up.

"Do you think I am dragging you two with me?" Pri was indignant. "For the record, I am not. I just reverse time, and you two being the time crawlers get drawn with me. You somehow remember the previous loops, while normal humans don't."

"All right. But this time, we go with a plan." Rigasur placed his hands on the table and eyed both of them.

"Why would I listen to you?"

"Tej, will you knock some sense in your daughter?"

Pri smirked.

Tej looked at Pri. She had a frown on her face, slouching rebelliously. She was full of hatred and anger, but no clue what to do with it.

"Rig, will you give both of us a minute?"

"With pleasure. I will go talk to Venkat, see if I can prevent the zombie girl from leveling us this time." Rigasur stormed out.

"I guess a lecture is coming." Pri looked at Tej in anger.

"Okay, listen to me—"

"Why? Why should I listen to even a single word you have to say? Because you are my father? What is one thing you have done for me as a father?" Pri's face turned red.

Tej gulped.

"You abandoned me when I was a kid. I was lost to God knows where. Trikaaldevi brought me back, gave me a few powers. But I still grew up without parents in a strange land. Can you imagine how life was for an orphaned kid? If anything, I owe it to Trikaaldevi. Not to you." She got up and pointed her finger in his face. "You are nothing to me."

Tej could not speak. He knew she was hurting on the inside. He cleared his throat. "So, that's what this is about?"

"You're damn right it is."

"I, your father, abandoned you. You are right. But do you know what my father tried to do? He and his brother raped and tortured my mother throughout my childhood. And as if that wasn't enough, they tried to kill me when I was eight. Imagine the kind of scars that leaves on a child."

Pri stood, shaken. She knew Tej had trapped Kumbh, but she did not know these details.

An uncomfortable silence swept across the room.

Pri started speaking again. She was failing to hold back her tears. "But you had your mother, who loved you and cared for you. And then you had your vengeance."

"Yes, my mother loved me. But taking revenge on my father did not heal those scars. Those wounds remain, Pri. Because I know wherever my father is, he will never love me as his child. Any opportunity he gets to hurt me, he will take it without a thought."

Pri was looking down at the ground, sobbing.

Tej walked up to her and clasped her shoulders. "Though I will never get my father back, you have a chance to get yours. I am here. And I swear, I am never going to leave you again."

"Why should I believe you? You left me before; you will do it again. Do you remember that I gave you my bangles? You said you would come back with them. You broke your promise to your little girl. Why would you keep it now?"

Tej was overwhelmed with emotion. He cupped Pri's face in his hands. "I was a nobody at that time. I knew nothing about my powers, about the world of time demons, time readers, and Kshins. I didn't know what I was getting into. I was a child in the skin of a man. Now having lived hundreds of lives, I know a lot more. And you and your mother, I missed both of you so much. Your non-existence left a void in my heart I just couldn't fill. Believe me, Pri, when I say these words. I will never let it happen again."

Pri hugged him tightly and burst into tears.

Tej hugged her and patted her back. "Never again, kiddo, never again."

Pri calmed down and wiped her tears.

"Now listen to me, kid. We need to believe in Rigasur. And we need to listen to him."

"But—"

"I know. He has his flaws, and he has a very dark past. But I have full faith that he has turned himself around. I could have never won over Nefe had he not been on my side. He is resourceful, sharp, and we need every bit of his scheming brain if we want to win over this formidable enemy, Tamas. Do you trust me enough to follow me in this battle without doubting my or Rig's decisions?"

Pri looked into his eyes. "I trust you, Dad."

Tej smiled.

11:27 AM, Launch site

Tej, Pri, and Rig stood at the middle of the platform.

"Why can't we stop Nancy from coming here?" Pri whispered to Rigasur.

"She is a walking talking time bomb. Tamas can trigger it at any time. And he would be tracking her coordinates. If we don't allow her here, Tamas will trigger here wherever she is. Let her come here. We know for sure when she will make her move. We will deal with her at the right time."

"This better work. I don't think I can reverse time again anytime soon. I thought I could, but I feel weak inside."

"Stay tight, stay on course. Just follow the plan."

Pri nodded.

Johaan and Mathur were setting up their laptops. Obelius stood playing around with the bow.

Venkat came back and ranted about the politician. He then looked at Pri and smiled. "I have a surprise for you." He pointed to an armored car speeding towards them.

"Oh, okay." Pri feigned ignorance but felt weak in her gut. *How could Nancy do this? How did Tamas convert her?*

The car stopped near the edge of the platform. The door at the back opened and Nancy came out.

Rigasur tilted his head a little, signaling Pri.

"Nancy!" Pri jumped with fake joy, ran towards her, and hugged her. Nancy kissed her forehead as they parted.

"You're back in your strange dress?" Pri sniggered. Each atom of her was revolted, but she had to keep the fake face until Rigasur signaled.

Pri and Nancy conversed, and then she introduced Nancy to Tej and Rigasur.

"All right, fellas. We are ready." Venkat's voice caught their attention.

Obelius had placed the arrow on the bow and was in the right position. The Samyantak was glowing brightly.

"Okay, now I will connect to our networks for thirty seconds, for last-minute checks." Johaan Pressed some keys on his laptop. Obelius, when I give a thumbs up, you fire."

"Noted!" Obelius tightened her pull on the string and stretched it to the end. All the muscles in her body were tense.

Rigasur looked at Pri and Tej. The time for Nancy's turning was near.

Johaan licked his lips in anxiety. "For us to make sure that Brahm-Astra's path is completely clear we would need to connect to the intranet for thirty seconds." His balding forehead was drenched with sweat. "Our thirty seconds begin now!"

30…29…28…

"Weather patterns, clear. Air-traffic movement, nil."
26…25…24…

"Obelius, you are good to go." Johaan raised his thumb.
19…18…17…

Obelius pulled it an inch back and was about to release it when a muffled explosion was heard at a distance.

"Tej, now!" Rigasur screamed.

Tej closed his eyes and concentrated. When he opened, his eyes were glowing sparkling blue.

Everyone around them now stood straight with their eyes glowing blue. Venkat, Johaan, Mathur, Nancy, CIPF soldiers, everyone: Tej had possessed all of them.

Pri looked around and chuckled. "You're good."

Obelius wasn't possessed and stood frozen.

"Tej why did you not possess this giant?" Rigasur demanded.

"Nancy and Obelius both have overly complex super-soldier brains. If I possess both along with hundreds of other people I am currently possessing, I can just keep them still. I won't have enough juice to have them take any action." Tej stood straight too as if trying to balance a ton of load on his head.

"What's happening?" Obelius asked.

Rigasur smiled. "Nothing. You go ahead and shoot the Brahm-Astra." The situation was deviating from what he planned.

"I won't move a muscle until you tell me what the hell is happening," Obelius thundered.

"What do we do now, Rig?" Pri was nervous.

Suddenly, a five-inch-long tranquilizer dart came flying and hit Obelius in the neck. Obelius stumbled and dropped to her knees, then came crashing down, along with the bow—crushing the surface beneath her.

22
NOW THEY COME FOR ME

Rigasur rubbed his forehead and murmured, "Damn. Tamas is prepared for every possibility."

"You said you had a perfect plan," Pri mocked.

"Oh yeah, no plan is perfect. Let me think."

"We are losing the Brahm-Astra launch window."

"You possess Obelius."

"What? But she is unconscious, perhaps dead."

"I know. Use your time demon energy and lift her. Do it!"

Pri closed her eyes. She slumped to the ground.

Obelius' eyes opened with a pink glow. She slowly stood up and curled her fingers into a fist. "So much strength." She clenched her teeth and pulled out the tranquilizer dart and threw it away. She looked at Rigasur. "Now what?"

Rigasur looked at Nancy's armband. It was blinking rapidly. "Tamas triggered her. She is gonna explode." He looked at Obelius. "Pri, throw Nancy as far away as possible, preferably in the ocean."

"Smart!" Obelius chuckled. She walked towards Nancy and clasped her by her left leg, lifting her several feel up in the air as if she weighed nothing. She then tilted herself back and threw Nancy away like a toy. Nancy's body leaped several hundred feet in the air and disappeared into the ocean waters with a tiny splash.

"That takes care of the bomb." Rigasur gazed at the portion of the ocean where her body dropped. He turned to Pri. "Launch the Brahm-Astra asap. Coordinates must already be set into your eye-lens. Shoot the damn arrow, and let's get this over with."

Obelius picked up the bow, the Samyantak glowed. She placed the arrow and pulled back the string. She was ready to shoot the arrow.

There was another muffled explosion, this time near them. Rigasur watched in awe as a hundred feet high tide rose in the ocean where Nancy's body fell. The bomb had exploded inside the water. The ominous tide, which looked like a wall of water, traveled towards them at immense velocity.

"Do it, Pri, it's now or never!" Rigasur clenched his fists.

Pri let go of the string. The Brahm-Astra arrow left the bow and rose higher, barely touching the top boundary of the gigantic tide, and flew away unchecked.

"Tej, let go of your possession!" Rigasur shouted.

Tej closed his eyes and took a deep breath. Everyone around them slowly came back to their senses.

Tej, Pri, and Rigasur watched in horror as millions of gallons of water swept across the area, submerging, men, machines, and buildings. They could hear the noise of military choppers fast approaching, help was coming.

As hundreds of bodies tried to swim to the surface in the turbulent waters, waiting to be rescued, the Brahm-Astra was fast disappearing in the sky.

A few seconds later, a loud sonic boom resounded in the area.

Twenty-two thousand feet below Wuhanzu City, China
Ten seconds later

In a large underground cuboidal chamber was situated a six-foot-high and twenty-foot-long oval water tank with a white dolphin swimming into it. The dolphin swirled to the depth of the tank and then came to the edge of the tank. She peeped at a large TV screen, which showed a red blinking dot on black background.

The chamber's door opened, and an eight-foot-tall humanoid robot walked in. Its metallic body of tungsten carbide glistened under the ceiling light, and its muscles made of elastic carbon fiber flexed. It walked and stood at the edge of the water tank where the dolphin gazed at the television screen.

"You couldn't prevent the launch." A hoarse whistle-like noise emanated from the dolphin's throat.

The robot stood quiet. Then he walked near to the dolphin, patted her head, and placed his hand below the fish's beak, caressing the skin.

"Your bomb exploded underwater," the dolphin spoke again. "Did anyone survive?"

"Some humans did, soldiers mostly. And time crawlers would have. They always do." The robot kept looking at the TV screen. "They are near-immortal."

"What happens now?"

"They saved the planet." The robot paused. "For now."

"We took our best shot and missed. Now it's their turn. It's time to relocate to the beta-side." The dolphin swam back to the other end of the tank.

The robot stood there for a moment and walked out.

Three days later, 29th February 2080, Vladivostok, Russia

Two mafia men in large overcoats, wearing black woolen monkey masks, walked through small lanes of a dingy suburb. These two men were possessed by Tej and Rigasur.

Local Time was 23:37 hours. The lights on the streets were dim; the ground was sticky with rain. The houses on each side of the street looked the same. with no house numbers. Most of them had no light switched on. An occasional flickering street-light bulb illuminated an otherwise clouded night.

Rigasur whispered as he sped up and turned lanes sharply. "Pri should have come with us. How will she learn the ways of the time demons?"

"Ways of time demons? Really?"

"I mean the way we do stuff. She has been a normal human for far too long. It's high time she realizes her powers."

"I was a normal human for the first twenty-four years of my life. I turned out to be your run-of-the-mill time demon."

Rigasur shrugged.

Tej continued, with a sadness in his voice, "She's seen enough. Some time-off would do her good."

"Hah, their lives were doomed the moment Venkat let that zombie step onto their military base. A severe security lapse, if you ask me." Rigasur slowed down near a cluster of houses at the end of the lane. "This is it."

"How do you even...."

"Shhh!" Rigasur signaled Tej. He then walked up to a wall and knocked it three times.

Tej could tell that his knock had a specific rhythm to it.

A rectangular door-size patch of the wall slightly changed color and turned light grey. Rigasur inserted his hand inside the patch, then his body, and vanished inside.

Tej shook his head. *Another secret door.* He followed, but as he stepped inside, he stood in the pitch dark. Then he heard Rigasur's voice addressing someone at a distance. He spoke in Russian, but Tej could understand it. "Kazimir, let him in, he's with me."

A sharp ceiling light illuminated the entire room. Tej looked around and felt as if he had traveled to the mid-nineteenth century. He was in a small room with dim green lights illuminating the edges where the ceiling met the walls. It was tough to ascertain where the light came from. Large, dusty cardboard boxes were kept all around the room. On one corner lay a small dirty bed with a crumpled bedsheet, and on the other was established a mega computer station with seven laptops, three big TV screens, a mesh of various wires, and router-like equipment. Clad in a red sweater, a middle-aged man with a balding head was sitting on a comfortable chair and was typing on one of the laptops rapidly. Rigasur stood next to him, smiling.

Tej couldn't see his face, and when he tried to walk towards the computer station, Rigasur signaled him to stay put. He then spoke loudly. "Kazimir, meet my friend, Tej. Tej, meet Kazimir, the world's best networking expert. Creator and destroyer of artificial intelligence."

Kazimir turned his head and looked at Rigasur. He spoke in a thick Russian accent. "Shut up your filthy mouth, Rig. Your flattery is not going to earn you any brownie points. I give you this, and we are done. I owe you nothing beyond that."

Rigasur was unfazed by this verbal attack as if he was half-expecting it. "Oh, come on, we go way back."

Kazimir grunted. He tapped out the side of his laptop and pulled out a one-inch-long shining pin. "This is your anti-AI."

Rigasur carefully took the pin and studied it. "This minuscule pin will take out the uber-powerful Tamas?"

"This is not a mere pin!" Kazimir roared. He sipped a hot liquid from a mug and continued, "This is a D.S.A.P. Distributed Scrambler Attack Protocol. It fires a series of continuous questions and false decisions towards an A.I., asking it to make a random decision at all times. Any A.I. would be compelled to answer these questions or negate these decisions."

"But an A.I. would very soon identify those patterns," Tej interrupted.

Both Rigasur and Kazimir looked at him as if they registered his presence in the room for the first time.

"Yes, but even most advanced A.I. will tackle such attack within half of a millisecond. To counter that, D.S.A.P. will keep changing the attack strategy every hundred microseconds. The victim A.I. will be lost in the barrage of continuous query attacks, and will be rendered incapable of taking any other decisions."

"So DSAP. is an A.I. too." Tej was lost in thought.

"Your friend is smart." Kazimir turned back to his screen.

"He is." Rigasur was impressed. "But how do we..."

"Sorry I did not print an instruction manual for you!" Kazimir roared again. "This pin has to be inserted in the networking port of the central server which hosts the A.I. The next time the A.I. resets across all its copies, the procedures will pass through the server. That is when this virus will begin its attack."

"I think we have what we came for." Rigasur smiled ear-to-ear.

"Yeah, time for you to get lost!" Kazimir jerked his arm and pointed his finger to the door.

Rigasur signaled Tej and they were about to talk out when Kazimir shouted, "Wait! Come here. This seems to be a message for you."

Both of them slowly approached the computer station. All the screens were showing grainy footage.

A background voice crackled through the mega speakers attached to the computer station. "I anticipated that you would come for me, so I have a surprise for you. Let me show you something."

A projector whirred on top of the room one of the bare walls on their left illuminated with a blue screen.

The screen size was twelve feet long and eight feet high.

"He's taken complete control of my networks and systems." Kazimir sat dejected in his chair.

"You have a wall projection system?" Rigasur was slightly amused.

Tej gave him a sharp look and Rigasur's smile vanished. This was a serious situation, and Tej couldn't understand the reason Rig was being so chirpy about it.

The footage began showing on the wall with the current date and time on the top left. It was a live stream possibly from a drone camera flying several thousand feet up in the air. It initially showed a picture of a mountain range and a plane flying at a distance. The camera slowly zoomed towards the plane it was a C-42KR, a military cargo carrier plane. The back ramp of the plane was fully open, where a mechanical setup was visible.

The camera further zoomed in to show an arrow mounted on a bow. The bow was held by a mechanical robotic arm that came down from the roof. Various chips were attached at several locations on the bow and the arrow from which wires were going down to the plane's ramp and the side walls.

"Is that a Brahm-Astra arrow?" Rigasur gasped.

"Yes, it is," Tamas's voice responded. "I wanted to thank you Tej and Rig for going the extra mile on this and getting me the schematics for this immensely powerful weapon."

The camera further zoomed to show the tip of the arrow and a blinking mechanical Samyantak.

Tej and Rig shared a glance.

"This was your plan all along, wasn't it?" Tej addressed Tamas. "You turned that asteroid towards Earth because you wanted us to find a weapon strong enough to destroy it. Then you stole the schematics and built your own."

"Well, that wasn't the plan all along, but I improvised along the way. I attempted to disrupt the launch but failed. Not sure how you survived my attacks, but you did. I did feel sad. That asteroid would have wiped out a major chunk of life on Earth and made my life easier. But now with this weapon, I can clinically aim and destroy whichever continent I want. I am on the same success path as I was before."

"You are bluffing," Tej snapped. "You can't fire this weapon."

"Are you alluding to the fact that I need a human being to fire this? I have solved that problem as well. The wires you see around the arrow are replicating the human pulse feedback loop. That is why you see the powerhouse, the Samyantak glowing."

Tej was thinking on his feet. Their momentous victory was turning towards a mammoth strategic defeat. "The weapon won't gain speed at this altitude. I have seen the schematics," he blurted out.

"Oh, this footage is just for display for you and some world-leaders. For the actual launch, I am evaluating satellite-based options. Don't think the threat is empty, gentlemen."

Rigasur wasn't amused. "Alright, go ahead, destroy the world. What are you waiting for?" This was serious, and he needed to know Tamas's intentions.

"Well, you two-time crawlers have been creating a lot of nuisance for me. I want you two out of the equation. I want both of you to surrender to me unconditionally."

"Or you'll destroy a continent. That's the threat here?" Rigasur almost rolled up his sleeves. The enemy was now out in the open, at least with his intentions.

"No. That's the eventuality. I have a little personal incentive for you to comply with."

The screen switched to a room illuminated with dim yellow light. A silhouette of a woman was visible. Chains wrapped around her wrists were stretching her arms up to the roof. Her lips were duct-taped, and her head was covered with chips and circuitry.

Tej took a hard look at the girl's face. His forehead tensed, his jaws tightened, and a feeling of rage ran across his spine.

The girl in the footage was Pri.

23
ABORT

Pri was alive. Very few people knew that Venkat, Pri, Minhas, and several other soldiers were saved in the deluge which swept across Sri Hari Kota on the day of the Brahm-Astra launch.

Tamas's voice echoed in the room. "I think she's important to you. Now that you have some skin in the game, here are my demands. You two will unconditionally surrender to me."

"Just because you have Pri means nothing. She is a time demon. She's immortal," Rig quipped.

"Are you sure?" Tamas's voice had sharp ridicule.

Tej gulped as the screen showed two small shining spheres slowly flying towards Pri. The spheres reached her and slowly started revolving around her. Tej had never seen the Z-bombs fly at such a controlled pace.

"You are well aware of what these tiny Z-bombs can do. The vortices these spheres generate can engulf any matter, including time-demons. And I have made some adjustments of my own, through which I control their velocities."

"What do we need to do?" Tej was humbled.

"After this video ends you will receive coordinates on this computer terminal. It's an abandoned parking lot in which a driverless fly-car with two dead-bodies is parked. You two need to possess those bodies and the car will bring you two to me. To a normal human, I would have given twelve hours, but your species is super-fast. So, you have just one minute. If you don't meet this timeline, she dies. Your one minute starts now."

The voice died down and a reverse digital timer appeared on the screen. 59…58…

"One minute?" Beads of perspiration appeared on Tej's forehead.

56…55…

Rigasur sank in his chair and closed his eyes.

Tej stood up. He was furious. This was the time Rig chose to leave them? But Rigasur opened his eyes after two seconds. "I know where is Tamas holed up."

"How?"

"Doesn't matter, Tej."

51…50…

"You just traveled in the past and met a time-reader, didn't you?"

"And then I came back to two seconds later. It was a tough jump, kid; I usually don't do it. Let's not waste time. Let's surrender both of us."

"No! You did good, Rig. I have an idea of mine." Tej looked at the timer.

42…41…

"I'll possess both bodies."

"You gotta be joking, Tej. He can detect our signature with high accuracy. That's how I think he tracked Pri."

"I can mess up with his signature device. Don't worry." Tej sat down and closed his eyes.

"Are you sure?" Rigasur noticed Tej's host's body stood still. He walked to it and touched it. The body slumped into the chair. "He's gone." He turned towards Kazimir. "He bought me time."

"I never thought I would be hacked. Ever." Kazimir let out a sad sigh.

"Ah, don't beat yourself up on this. There's always a first time for everything." Rigasur looked around the room. "Tell me, is there a circuit camera in this room that is not connected to any network?"

Kazimir pointed to a small red blinking dot in the north-west corner of the room.

A smile floated on Rigasur's face.

After possessing dead bodies, Tej opened his eyes. He realized that his hosts were blindfolded, and their hands were tied in front as they sat on comfortable seats. He could also feel a heavy helmet on the heads of both his hosts.

As soon as he possessed the bodies the car's engine whirred into motion. Tej could feel the vehicle rising into the air when a painful electric shock ran through his whole body. He lost consciousness.

Indian army secret base, Maxtrot-44

Venkat sat in front of a giant TV screen in a large conference room. At his side was Dr. Minhas, who stood smiling. Rigasur had again possessed him.

Venkat tilted towards him and whispered, "General Griffin still does not know that you are Rig and not Minhas. Do we want to keep up this play?"

"It's better that he does not know that us time crawlers are involved. We do not have a good rep anywhere in the world."

Venkat eased back into his chair. Venkat strongly believed that powerful alliances were built on trust and no secrecy.

The TV screen in front of them flickered and they both stood attentive. They could now see the smiling face of General Griffin talking directly to them, but they couldn't hear him.

"We can't hear you, General. Can you hear us?" Venkat spoke loudly. He then muttered, "Damn this old tech, we are short on time and we can't even connect."

They could see General turn to his side and scold a technician. It took a few minutes before they could converse.

"I am sorry for the technical issues, gentlemen." Griffin smiled. "I remember this VoIP was always this frustrating until we moved to quantum comm-tech in 2045. But today, we must go back to these archaic communication mechanisms, because however rusted this is, it's tougher for Tamas to hack our feed."

"No worries, General."

"So, if I am hearing you right, you are telling me that not only do you have the location of Tamas, but you also have some of your operatives inside his hideout?"

"Yes sir, but our operatives as of now are hostages."

"So, we can't rain down hell on that hideout and take Tamas down."

Venkat looked at Rigasur and then back at General. "Well, General, these operatives of ours are special individuals. They will slip out before you turn this place to ash."

"Interesting. I would like to know more about these special operatives. But that's a talk for later. From the coordinates that Dr. Minhas relayed, I gather that the Tamas is holed up in an ancient fort right at the centroid of the Sahara Desert."

"Yes."

"All right then. We have a destroyer, USS Mariela stationed in the territorial waters of Oman. Three F-536 Blitzkrieg-Hawk fighter planes will be airborne in exactly two minutes. ETA to target is fifteen minutes."

A nervous smile appeared on Venkat's face. "That's super-fast action, General. It seems you released the orders for a hit before you even talked to us."

The general let out a sardonic laugh, but his face bore an angry look. "Lt-General Venkat, Tamas has cost us money, time, and resources, but above all, Tamas has cost us lives. Several good American men and women, soldiers, and scientists, the best of our best, have sacrificed their lives in our fight against this evil AI. Any chance we get to hit this son-of-a-bitch, we gotta take it."

Arobaini grey-stone castle
Deep in Sahara Desert, North Africa

Tej opened his eyes in a dim-lit room, with small yellow flickering bulbs hung from the ceiling. He realized he was now inside Tamas's hideout. A light mist spread throughout the room further blurred his vision.

Both his host bodies stood with their hands pulled apart, tied to the roof, their feet barely touching the ground. Pitch black nano-particle tapes covered their lips and heavy helmets armored with electronic circuitry rested on their heads.

Tej winced to see Pri strung up in the same manner with a black tape on her lips and a similar helmet on her head. The circuit on the helmet buzzed with occasional sparks of electricity. Weak enough to keep the host alive, but strong enough to prevent a time-crawler from escaping.

He wanted to speak, but he knew that the more he tried to, the more the nano-particle tape would tie itself more to his skin.

Before Tej could think of anything, a sharp voice echoed through the room, "Tej. We finally meet in person."

Through the flickering blub and the light mist, Tej could make out a silhouette of a large, muscular man walking towards them. A red rectangle of light was visible on this man's face, in a place where men usually had eyes.

Through the mist emerged the body of a muscular robot, nine feet high and three feet wide. The robot's face was a straight metal semi-elliptical shape with a slight semblance to a human face. In place of the eyes was a shining rectangle filled with a red light. In place of lips were three vertical empty slots placed a quarter-inch apart. The robot's biceps, torso, legs, and almost all muscles were built of blue cold-rolled steel, with a thin layer of tungsten carbide giving it an extra shine. Wherever the steel limbs met at the folds or the torso, the body was joined by a complex but organized mesh of pitch-black carbon fiber. The left arm of the robot was thicker than the right because a small computer screen was embedded into it. All in all, the robot looked like a paranormal wrestler from a dystopian realm where machines had overtaken men.

Tamas bent down and brought his face close to Tej. "I know what you are thinking. You are planning. Scheming. 'How should I possess this robot? How do I make him do my bidding?' That's what you time crawlers do. You possess and you rule."

Tej grunted.

The robot stood straight and walked over to Pri.

Tej grunted again, this time louder.

"Don't worry. I will not harm her. If you keep cooperating, as you have been, she will stay safe."

Tej shook his head vigorously, and both his hosts did that together.

Tamas tilted its head as he looked at them. "How did this happen? Is this the rare phenomenon of multi-possession?"

Tej gulped. He had given away the secret.

Tamas lifted his left arm, and his right hand started pushing some buttons on the touch screen. "Ah, the time crawler signature is different. But if I run a different interpretation algorithm, the signals are nighty-nine percent similar. You cheated Tej. You cheated!" Tamas screamed.

It stretched out its left arm towards one of Tej's hosts and tilted his wrist downward. A small cylindrical nozzle appeared from under his gadget. With a sharp noise, a blue flame emerged from the nozzle and bathed one of Tej's host in flames.

Owing to the helmet, Tej couldn't pull out of the host and cringed in immense pain. His whole body writhed and struggled in the agony of third-degree burns. Within a few seconds, though, the helmet too caught fire, and he pulled out of that host. He slipped into unconsciousness.

Seventy miles away,
five thousand feet up in the air.

Three F-536 fighter jets sped towards their target in battle formation. Squadron leader Rebecca Bharara let the charge. Her plane's computer was giving her all the stats, but beyond her jet's window shield and through a light cloud cover, she could see the enlarging figure of the mammoth Arobaini castle in front of her. From seventy miles away, the castle looked like muddy wreckage in the middle of a shining golden ocean of endless sand.

Though the computer displayed a firearm deployment strategy, Rebecca was mentally calculating the firepower needed to destroy the gargantuan stone fort, its walls, and minarets. She always re-checked the computer's calculation. After a few seconds, she picked up her comm device and started speaking.

"Marble leader to Markov. We are going in hot, ETA seventy-five seconds."

General Griffin's digitized voice came through. "Markov to Marble leader. You are authorized to fire at will. Burn the hell out of the code-bug. Godspeed."

Rebecca put her comm-device down and focused. Her F-536 tilted a little and came down several hundred feet, breaking formation, and then sped faster.

The other two F-536s also broke formation one by one and followed Rebecca.

Inside the castle, Tej woke up coughing, still in pain. The feeling of burning flames peeling off his skin and corroding his flesh still haunted him. This was the second time in the past few days he suffered being burnt alive. He caught his breath and looked around.

Tamas stood in the same location. His left arm was stationed in a vertical stance in front of its body. A small device was projecting live footage onto the mist in front of him.

Tej too could see this live feed. It was three black dots thousands of feet up in the air, getting larger with time. *Rig did his job.*

"I see that your friends have sent a cavalry to save you." Tamas turned his head towards Tej. "I was getting worried for you, but it seems there is hope for you after all."

Tej grunted.

"Oh, I forgot, you can't speak." Tamas pressed a button on his gadget and swiped his metallic finger.

A small slit appeared in the tape on Tej's lips. Tej puked for the next few seconds.

"Take your time. Meanwhile, I have a small gift for your friends." Tamas touched the side of its head with his right hand and spoke.

With the drool still dripping off his chin, Tej looked up. Tamas was speaking a strange language as if he was issuing commands to someone.

US Air force secret headquarters, Oregon, United States

General Griffin was gulping down his seventeenth cup of coffee for the day. In front of him, a television screen was divided into two parts. The left part showed a world map schematic where three blue dots were approaching a red target. The right part showed live cam footage. He was seeing what Squadron leader Rebecca was seeing.

There was a knock on the door, and a lieutenant entered the room and saluted. He was drenched in sweat and was gasping for air.

"Not now!" the general roared. "What instructions did I leave?"

"We received something via rapid-mail. This could not wait, sir." He inserted a small magnetic drive into a computer terminal and pressed a few keys. A video began playing on the general's screen.

General Griffin's eyes were full of horror. "Connect me to Marble Leader right away!"

Five hundred feet up in the air, three miles away from Arobaini Castle

Rebecca had armed the inferno-XM23 missiles and was ready to fire. She planned a first damning wave of attacks after which the F-536s would go past the castle, then gain substantial attitude to prevent any anti aircraft retaliation. She then planned to come down and crush any remaining structure.

She dived to three hundred feet and was about to press her thumb when her comm device throttled. She clenched her teeth and answered the comm.

"Markov to Marble Leader! Abort!" General Griffin's voice was loud, clear and full of panic.

"What?" Rebecca scoffed.

"Abort, I repeat, Abort. Return to the alpha point and await new instructions!" The voice died.

Rebecca changed the frequency and shouted. "Abort, everyone, abort. We are leaving via exit routes Meet at the alpha rendezvous point. I repeat, abort, meet at alpha."

She put the comm down and banged her fist on her console. She let out a scream of immense frustration and then started to maneuver her fighter jet to gain altitude.

All three F-536s flew over the castle, gained altitude, and disappeared into the clouds.

Arobaini castle

Tamas turned towards Tej as both of them heard the bypass and then fading noise of F-536 fighters.

"Humans and their weaknesses. One video footage from me and they dropped the idea of attacking me."

Tej kept silent.

Tamas walked out of the room.

Tej heard a familiar voice inside his head.

Dad, can you hear me?

He looked at Pri. She was unconscious. "Pri, is that you? Where are you?"

Shh, Dad, don't speak. Communicate with your thoughts.

"Okay." Tej just thought of the word.

"Great, I can hear you loud and clear." Pri's voice sounded ecstatic. "Now close your eyes and follow my voice."

"But, where are you?"

"I am inside Tamas's mainframe. Since you are also connected to it, I can communicate with you."

Tej closed his eyes. "What do you mean, inside?"

"Try not to be shocked. I have hacked into Tamas."

"What?"

24
WARRIORS OF TAMAS

Cej opened his eyes. He was inside the body of an old man wearing a white gown. This man was hunkered beneath a table inside a small room. The floor and furniture were shaking due to frequent loud explosions from outside.

Next to him crouched a woman in her late twenties, who was dressed as a soldier. She had a shotgun in her hand. She was on her toes, keenly trying to hear for movement outside.

"Pri is that you?"

"Yes, Fad."

"Which place on Earth is this? I was not aware of any active war zones in 2080."

"Not a place on Earth—we are inside *Warriors of Tamas*, a massively multiplayer role-playing game, an MMORPG. It's played in virtual reality all over the world by thousands of elite users via darknet connections."

"So, we are in VR."

"Yes. Only best of the best players are allowed to enter this post-apocalyptic world where cities lay in ruin and machines rule the world."

An explosion close by shook the entire room violently. A few bricks along with dirt came crashing down from the roof.

"This looks so real. This room, these explosions. Why the hell is Tamas hosting an MMORPG? And why are we in it?"

"Tamas is protecting something."

"What?"

Pri put her shotgun down and clicked on a rectangular gadget tied to her left wrist. A small 3D-projection map with criss-cross roadways opened up with a small blue dot blinking in the middle. "This is what he is protecting. It's a self-destruct trigger, built by Andrele when he first designed Tamas. This trigger was scheduled to go off sometime in the 2070s. But by then, Tamas had evolved. He placed it inside a virtual reality so that…"

"… the clock does not tick," Tej completed. "Time-absent zones within a VR."

"Exactly!"

"But why create a game around it? He could have buried it into deep dark-web."

"A game creates motion, and motion creates time, which balances the time-absent zones. A VR with all time-absent zones will be highly unstable."

Tej paused. "So, all the human players plugged into the MMORPG, they have a target to bring this blue dot down?"

"Not all of them. Some are attackers, others are defenders. Needless to say, the way they are chosen, attackers are much weaker at playing this game than the defenders. The game is heavily rigged."

"Why do we need to go through this rigged game?" Tej looked at Pri with anticipation. "You said you've hacked into Tamas. Can't you bring him down?"

Pri looked at him as if he said something stupid. "No chance. Tamas is an impregnable AI with inbuilt fortifications that make it virtually impossible to hack it from inside or outside. This VR is the only chink in his armor."

"So, if we win this game, Tamas is gone?"

"That's a very big if. I am barely surviving inside this MMORPG, slowly moving towards this blue dot. Tamas has detected that I am inside, but can't exactly locate me. That is why he's directing his defenders to bomb this place down."

"But he has Z-bombs. He can extinguish you from existence any time he wants!"

Pri's character made a noise similar to a smirk. "He had only one, which he used for the attack on Brahm-Astra launch. He does not have any more of them. If he threatened you with them, he was bluffing. Zason-bombs are extremely hard to manufacture. I found some archives in his database which showed he experimented with them but failed."

Tej paused. Pri being on the inside was bringing out Tamas's weaknesses. A series of explosions nearby broke his thought.

Pri's ears were tuned to noises from outside. "They're close. We should move. We need to reach this blue dot, and need to eliminate any defenders who are in our path."

"Eliminate? What happens if a human player's avatar gets killed?"

"They are out of the game."

"Oh, okay."

Tej focused his vision and could see some stats rolling down in front of his eyes.

Intelligence: 28/100

Power: 5/100

Agility: 7/100

Weapons: None

Player Level: Novice

He was indignant. "These game stats look weak to me. What character am I in?"

"Yeah, it is weak. You're inside a side-character. You need a new avatar, a real solid one if we need to elude him and attack that blue dot." She heard a missile fire. "We need to get out of this house, right now."

Pri moved fast and unbolted the door. Before Tej could crawl outside, she held his arm and dragged him out from beneath the bed. She sprinted out as fast as they could and Tej stumbled behind her. Before they could cover a few feet, a ball of fire from the sky struck the house they were in and incinerated it with a loud explosion. They were steered clear of the blast, but were caught in the immense shockwave that emanated from the house, and were flung further onto the ground, rolling into the mud.

Tej looked around and beyond the light mist, he could see broken buildings and burning houses. It was a world full of chaos and destruction. Above him, the sky was covered with dark clouds, with an occasional pass of a flying gunship.

"Your character is slowing me down, Dad. You need to find a new one." Pri looked around with her shotgun ready to fire.

"Not just any character, the best possible attacker this game has."

Pri touched Tej's hand, and he could see a username flash in front of his eyes.

Anderson1729ZZZ

"He's the second-best attacker in the game. You get into his avatar, there's no one stopping both of us."

"Second best? Who's got the best?"

"I have. You know what to do." Pri pressed a button and two large metallic wings spurted out of her back like an origami unfolding. She waved at Tej and flew down a narrow dark alleyway, disappearing in the mist.

Tej was about to get up when he heard loud gunfire near him. He looked down at his body and saw it ridden with bullet-holes and blood seeping out. He slumped onto the ground.

Jambavati District, Pune, India, a minute later

Rahul Nagrekar was a bulky nineteen-year-old who had spread himself on a comfortable sofa and was munching potato chips. He was surfing the internet on his laptop for cute cat pics when his eyes glowed pink. Tej had possessed him.

He quickly strapped on his virtual reality spectacles and fired up the Warriors of Tamas 3.0 app on his main screen. He logged in as Anderson1729ZZZ and started typing a message to another game user.

"Dad, here. I am in."

Tej then checked his new character's stats

Intelligence: 92/100

Power: 97/100

Agility: 99/100

Weapons: Arsenal level 747

Player Level: Star Player Elite

"That's more like it." Tej chuckled.

Indian army secret base, Maxtrot-44

Brigadier Venkat sprinted through a gallery with Rigasur behind him, trying to play catchup. Venkat was suited up in a dark purple military outfit and carried two short-ranged pistols, a shotgun, and several hand-grenades on him.

"Brigadier Venkat, can we sit and talk for five minutes? I will explain everything." Rigasur was gasping for air, and he jogged behind Venkat.

"We don't have time, Rig. You can tell me everything on my way. My super-soldier unit is waiting for me at the tarmac, and a carrier plane is ready to take us to Arobaini castle. We are storming that fortress now."

"Tej and Pri are inside a virtual reality multiplayer game. They think they have something which can destroy Tamas."

Venkat took the turn into the last gallery and rushed towards the main door of the facility. "I understand neither the world of time crawlers nor these VR games. All I know that we are going to storm this castle and get those children out. The more time we spend waiting, the higher the chance that we won't get our hostages alive."

Venkat bolted out the main door and sprinted towards a military plane at a distance. Rigasur was two feet behind him, trying to keep up, his legs getting tired.

"Brigadier, we should be careful not to jeopardize Tej and Pri's mission."

"What mission?" Venkat smirked. "Seems like fool-hardiness to me. Tamas can't be defeated from inside of an online game in a virtual cyber world. He is a real threat in our real world, and needs to be dealt with extreme force."

As they neared the military plane the silhouettes of Venkat's super-soldiers were more clearly visible. They were thirty women in their early twenties and wore the exact super-soldier outfit as Nancy earlier did.

"Nancy's clones?" Rigasur was surprised.

"No, not clones, each of them is a unique fighter. Do you think Nancy was the only super-soldier Indian Armed Forces sanctioned?" Venkat was proud and ecstatic. "Nancy was just a prototype. And after studying her flaws, we have improved their designs. Tamas can't hack into them. And if we are met with lethal force from Tamas's drones, these girls will tear them to pieces, by their own bare hands."

"Look Brigadier, can we…"

Venkat stopped and took a sharp turn. "Well Rig, you listen to me. In the short period that we've known each other, you have earned my respect. I can't say that for a lot of people. You are a smart strategist, and you may have an elaborate plan, but I can't be a pawn standing on the side, waiting for things to unfold. I have lost a lot of good people in this fight. And I will either take down the enemy or go down trying."

Rigasur stood silent.

Venkat calmed down. He realized he was pouring out on the wrong person. "Look why don't you play our quarterback here, our joint control room? Keep me updated about what Tej and Pri are doing. And I will keep the communication line open from my end. Let's view this as an attack from two fronts."

Venkat kept his gaze tight on Rigasur.

Rigasur nodded.

Venkat donned his eyeglasses and jogged onto the plane's ramp. All the super-soldiers followed them.

Rigasur waited till the plane took off and vanished into the azure.

Inside the Virtual Reality

Tej and Pri stood in front of a castle, which resembled Arobaini. Tej's character was now of a prince named *Rimodaan*. Eight feet high muscular man carrying a three feet long spectacular titanium sword. He wore a thick golden helmet and golden armor covered his whole torso. His legs were covered in orange trousers protected by disjointed flexible metal plates. Pri's fantasy game character was gleaming as well. She was princess *Iraka*, donned in a blood-red warrior dress, adorned with blue body armor and a serpent sign on her chest.

The castle in front of them was the location of the blue dot. They both had set their wrist gadget in a way that it showed a running digital game clock at all times.

"So, wherever this clock stops, we're close to a time-absent zone?"

Tej nodded. "I have some experience with time-absent VRs." He recalled his time when Mozeek pulled him out of the VR prison.

"Let's get the party started." Pri pointed her sword to the castle door, and a scathing streak of blue flames shot through it striking the door with a loud bang. A translucent reverse countdown beginning from ten thousand appeared on top of the door.

Tej's character jumped slightly and pointed his sword towards the sky. A streak of green lightning raced through his sword upwards and a series of periodic lightning bolts started hitting the castle door, weakening it even further. The reverse countdown sped faster.

As they damaged the castle door, Pri and Tej could see some shadows circling them from a distance.

"Here come the stupid-ass defenders. Dad, I'll keep damaging this door, can you take care of these rats?"

"With pleasure!" Tej brought his weapon down and switched a gear on the hood, his sword illuminated with a glistening yellow hue. He then flew several feet up and swept the blade in thin air, making a circular motion. A series of bright gleams of circular blazes flew outwards from him like wave patterns and struck the incoming defenders.

"I am enjoying this much more than I thought," he chuckled.

The Arobaini castle, real world

About 10.5 kilometers up in the air, Venkat was aboard the military plane, doing a last-minute briefing with his team. Their aim was a classic HALO approach, with their chutes opening roughly half a kilometer above the castle.

They planned to descend directly into the castle compound beyond the main door. All the soldiers in the team, including Venkat, were going to use GPS-enabled chutes so that their hands remain free to return enemy fire. Venkat was also anticipated to be attacked by electronically-controlled fully-automated weaponry; each soldier carried an additional EM pulse gun.

A massive on-ground US military unit was encircling the castle as they prepared for their HALO jump. Three hundred armored vehicles carrying heavy-mortar guns were approaching the castle from all directions. Five military choppers were on standby five miles back, planning to enter the conflict at a decisive moment later.

At exactly 10:55 hours, the US military began heavy shelling on the castle, giving a distraction cover fire to Venkat's team. Within five seconds, fourteen strategically-placed rotatory machine guns emerged from behind the top of castle walls and started returning fire. The twelve-barrel heavy-duty machine guns tied to wires were sliding and moving at 3D angles, fully controlled from the inside. And that was not all, the central dome of the castle opened from the top and twenty mega chopper drones emerged out of it one by one. The drones were supported by four rotatory blades and each of them was fitted with two miniaturized cruise-missiles. The drones took optimal positions and started firing the cruise missiles at specific locations blasting off the armored cars.

Major Josephine Garth of US-Airforce, who was monitoring the situation from USS Mariela destroyer two hundred miles away, was shocked at the enemy onslaught. The area had turned into a heated war zone, and it was clear that Tamas was well prepared for a long stand-off.

Three minutes later, at 10:58, Venkat switched on his comm device and relayed a cryptic message, "Grey Bird to Red Eagle, we are commencing ziplining into the horizon."

Major Josephine replied from the other end, "Fireworks are on, you are green to zipline. Be careful. Red Bird out."

Venkat switched off his comm, glanced at his team once, and jumped out of the plane ramp, nose-diving towards the ground. He was followed by his unit in groups of two.

Falling from thirty thousand feet up in the air, they planned to be in free-fall for three full minutes. One minute into the fall, while they all were straight-diving towards the ground, Lieutenant Sakshi adjusted a forty-inch-long EMP-bomb launcher on her shoulder and arm. She targeted it onto the centroid of the castle which was faintly visible from up there. The launcher looked more like a shiny metal tube with two black rubber buttons on one side. She pushed the buttons hard, and three copper balls shot out of the launcher's barrel one after the other.

The balls sped towards the castle. At about two kilometers above the fortress, three of them aligned in a horizontal formation, as if revolving around an invisible center in between them. There was a sharp spark right in the middle of the three revolving balls, and a severe electromagnetic pulse boomed in two square mile radius. Engines of all the armored cars shut off, and all communications were out. The automatic machine guns firing at US Armed Forces came to a standstill with their circuity fried. The drones firing cruise missiles also came down, crashing as their inner electrical system burned up. The three copper balls disappeared inside the castle compound harmlessly, but they had done their job.

Inside the castle, the power went out for a second, and then quickly came back, owing to backup generators, but half of the instruments inside were not working. Tamas walked up to a monitoring station and pressed a few buttons, running full system-diagnostics.

In the control room, Major Josephine banged her table loudly. "Gotcha, son-of-a-bitch." She picked up her radio and gave fresh orders. "Marble Leader to Desert Hawks, toys are down. Time to rain some fire."

Operators of five US Military helicopters, which were stationed three miles away, had received their orders. They lifted off and stormed towards the castle with their weapons red-hot to fire.

All this happened in a one-minute window, during which Venkat and his unit had covered a major part of their descent, and were barely four kilometers above the castle.

The military choppers came in hot and aimed at the twelve-barrel machine guns now sitting silent. After demolishing the guns, they also targeted the drones on the ground, turning them to ashes as well. As the choppers finished their quick in-and-out and turned back, Venkat's team was two kilometers above the castle. Their chutes opened, slowing them down with strong jerks. Within the next five minutes, they landed in an empty compound inside the castle.

The chopper noises were fading as they flew away, and the armored cars were turning around and falling back. Their job was done; the Indian military surgical unit had successfully infiltrated the castle.

Venkat and his unit found themselves staring at the entrance of a series of mazes, a set of doors, with no hint for which ones were a dead end and which not. Venkat divided the unit into several sub-teams and started a grid search of the castle. They anticipated further drone or robot attacks and were ready for any incoming onslaught.

Deep inside Arobaini Castle

Tamas was moving through various control rooms, trying to assess the damage the EMP pulse did. He entered the room where the lifeless hosts of Pri and Tej hung from ropes. He ignored them and walked over to a nearby chamber, where his pet dolphin swam in a large transparent oval tank.

"They've won this round." The dolphin's whistle-laden voice echoed through the room.

"The probability of the current scenario happening was 0.05%."

"Yet it happened. Time crawlers are working with humans, and together, their actions are unpredictable. You were not designed to combat paranormal entities."

Tamas stood quiet and then spoke in a much deeper, personal voice. "But I was designed to adapt and prevail."

"They are at your doorstep. What now?"

"A surprise will be waiting for them."

The dolphin took a deep breath above the surface. "Why not deploy the ancient weapons right away?"

"That's my last leverage. The probability of them succeeding here is still negligible. The VR battle will take all my focus."

Inside the Virtual Reality

While the outside world had just witnessed a heavy artillery fire exchange, Tej and Pri were thundering through their surroundings with some astounding magical weapons. They had not only demolished the castle door but were laying waste to anything or anyone who came in their path. Their superlative powers made them near-invincible in this game, and they had knocked hundreds of players out of the MMORPG in the last few minutes. Internet forums were abuzz over the sudden collaboration between two unstoppable players who were bringing their A-game. Defenders were joining chatrooms in hordes, sharing game clips, and devising new strategies.

Pri and Tej entered a long, shadowy tunnel and jogged towards the end. At the far end of the tunnel stood their ultimate target, the blue dot on the map.

"Why is Tamas letting us win? Why not change the rules of the game and knock us out?"

"While any minor changes can be done by changing web-based codes, for any major changes to the game, it would need a new patch and a possible restart. And any restart will remove all time-absent zones momentarily, causing the trigger to re-activate."

"Makes sense. Have you established a connection with Rig?"

"Yes, I have found a secure proxy connection embedded deep inside the game architecture. We can use that."

They sprinted to the far end of the hallway. They could now see a set of shadows at the very end. From a distance, they looked like children.

As they approached the end they slowed down and saw that a pack of fifty dwarves with blue swords stood in attack stance. Right behind the dwarves was a large brick-laden wall with circular metallic doors.

Tej noticed the digital clock on his wrist, the seconds counter was frozen.

"This is it, Pri. We are at the cusp of the time-absent zone. As soon as we blast through the door behind these dwarves, the time-absent zone will be destroyed, and..."

"...the self-destruct trigger will activate," Pri completed.

She was about to raise her sword when a strange voice echoed through the hallway. "Go ahead, use your magical weapon, but if you do so, the dwarves will throw themselves in the path of it and will die."

"No one dies in this game," Pri yelled back. She wasn't sure where the voice came from, but it demanded attention.

A translucent apparition of a wizard with a pale white face and dark robe appeared on their right.

Pri and Tej stole a glance.

Wizard spoke. "These are no dwarves; these are small children, who are currently my captives. But by all means, go ahead and kill these children in cold blood. Your time-demons have killed many innocent souls throughout the ages. Today would not be any different."

"How can they die?" Pri was getting pissed-off.

The wizard shifted on his feet. "Let me set some context up for you. All the other avatars you killed in this game were human players simply knocked out of the game. But these fifty dwarves in front of you are kids who are hooked to electric circuits, sleeping in sensory deprivation pools, inside the real castle. The moment you kill their avatars here, they die in the real world."

"You are a lying son of a bitch."

The wizard held his hands together. "Don't believe me; ask your beloved GI Joe. He's just about to breach the gates of the hall these children are in. I know you are connected to him."

Re-establishing her connection, Pri felt a lump in her throat. "Rig can you hear me? We need you to confirm something from the brigadier."

All of Venkat's sub-teams had trickled through the mazes and reached a large hall. As they carefully entered the hall with their weapons pointed to the front, the sensor-enabled ceiling lights switched on. In the mild blue light illuminating the hall, they could see in front of them fifty bathtubs, each filled with brown fluid, and a child floating in it. The children were all seven to ten years of age, and their heads were covered with a mesh of complex circuitry, with electrodes and wires going down below the tub into a strange switchboard.

Venkat signaled his team to spread out and study each of the tubs. He wasn't sure what to make of this situation. The lens in his eyes was relaying these images back to the control room. He pressed his earphone. "Rig, are you seeing this? Have you ever seen something like this before?"

Back at the control room, Rigasur was looking at the images. "I can see them, Brigadier. There are devices similar to the Concordia VX interfacing the human brain with a machine. They're wired into the system." He addressed Pri, "I am afraid it's not an empty threat; the children are here."

Inside the game, Pri and Tej had lowered down their weapons.

"So, you got the message." Wizard shifted on his feet. "Now let me tell you your options. Either you mercilessly cull these little beauties and go inside to trigger my end, or these well-trained kids kill both your avatars and knock you out of this game forever. And once they are done with you, I will pump the hall they are in with sarin gas, killing them and your beloved Brigadier Venkat."

Pri spoke loudly, "Rig, ask Brigadier sir to free the children right now."

"Not so fast. This is not the only card up my sleeve." The wizard pointed a finger at her. "If army-boy even touches the children, I will fire the two Brahm-Astra arrows right now. These arrows are mounted to two geo-stationary satellites right above New York and New Hastinapur. Millions, if not billions, will die."

In the Arobaini castle, the same message from Tamas echoed in the hall where Venkat and his team stood. He ordered his team to stay put and not touch anything in the room. This was a stalemate situation. Their hands were so close to Tamas's throat, yet the A.I. had them by their balls, and there was nothing they could do.

25
THE ENDGAME

Inside the VR world, the wizard had disappeared, and the dwarves were now ambling towards Tej and Pri, who were retreating with care.

Inside Arobaini, Venkat had signaled his team to stay where they were. He was torn between trying to save the innocent children or quickly exfil his team and cut back his losses. His super-soldiers did possess herculean strength, but were still humans, after all. He knew if sarin were released in this chamber, it would attack and paralyze their neuromuscular junctions, as it would do for any normal human being. He had noticed several nozzles on the roof pointing downwards, testimony to the fact that Tamas was not bluffing.

In the control room, Rigasur was hitting his forehead with his fist. Tamas was beating them every step of the way, and they just stood helpless.

"Rig." Tej's voice echoed through his laptop. "Guide us. You are the only one who can save the day."

"I am out of options too, Rig, unless you have something for me. No pressure, though." That was Venkat on the radio.

"No pressure," Rigasur smirked. This was what he was best at, finding ways out of tough circumstances. But this situation was turning into a complicated game of chess. Each move had several pros and cons, but the time was running out.

He closed his eyes and let the pieces of the puzzle fit in. He then opened them and shot back, "Brigadier, you and the team have ballistic weapons. Take out all the nozzles in the room."

"But...?"

"Do it!"

Venkat motioned to his team and started shooting at the nozzles. His team did the same. All the nozzles in the room were destroyed.

"Bravo, that takes out the sarin angle." Rigasur was now flexing his neck muscles.

"Idiots! You've committed the cardinal mistake." Tamas's voice roared in the hall where Venkat stood in. "Now you shall pay. I'll release the Brahm-Astras now. All the deaths are on you."

At the same time, inside virtual reality, the dwarves closing in on Tej and Pri pounced on them. A strange sword battle began where the dwarves made ferocious strikes but Tej and Pri played defensive. It was only a matter of time before they suffered enough injuries to be knocked out of the game.

Rigasur checked the satellite network and found two fast-moving objects racing towards Earth from geostationary orbit. Their projected targets were New York and New Hastinapur. Tamas had released the Brahm-Astras.

"Friends, the Brahm-Astras are coming in hot. They were shot from the geostationary height of 37000 kilometers, but simulation models estimate they will stabilize at the speed of Mach 343."

"Can't do the math, Rig. How much time do we have?" Pri screamed as she saved herself from a horde of dwarves raving to tear into her flesh.

"Time to impact would be more, but after three minutes, they will hit a critical path and be unstoppable. Buy some time, I'll come back to you."

2 minutes, 58 seconds to the critical path.
2:58…57…56…

Rigasur yelled, "Brigadier, switch to EM guns and fry the whole place! That will disable all the electronic circuitry."

"Are you sure, Rig? Firing the EM pulses won't kill the children?" Venkat and his team took out their EM pulse guns.

"Yes, I'm sure. These circuits are not embedded in their necks, they are outside. Go for it."

"You better be right. I don't want to be a child-killer!" Venkat yelled back.

"Do it, Venkat, fucking do it! We don't have time!" Rigasur stood at his seat, his throat parched, his hands digging into the wooden table in front of him.

Venkat and his team started firing the mini-EM pulses, directing them towards the circuity and switchboards as much as possible. Wherever the pulses hit, they could see the circuits spark and wires catching fire.

2:23…22…21…

Venkat and his team paused for two seconds, then immediately swung into action. They started removing the wire-meshes and pulled the kids out of tubs. Each super-soldier carried two children on each of their shoulders and stormed out of the hall, towards the castle entrance.

2:03...02...01...

Inside the virtual reality, the dwarves started vanishing in thin air, until Pri and Tej were left alone in front of the door. They immediately turned the combined might of their swords to the door, and it burst into pieces.

The virtual reality around them began to shake and distort. Their beautiful high-definition characters started to pixelate.

"Dad, Tamas is dying, and with him, his whole virtual world is going down." Pri dropped her sword. "Go ahead, leave this avatar, I will follow."

1:57...56...55...

"I won't leave you, Pri." Tej held her hand.

"Don't worry about me, Dad. I need to finish an important task before I exfil. I will see you soon."

"Are you sure you won't need me? I can stay." Tej was overwhelmed with emotions. He had that dreadful feeling that he was losing her all over again.

"I am sure. There's nothing you can do here."

1.43...42...41...

Tej started to close his eyes and could see Pri's character melting and dissolving into a pixelated liquid.

His eyes shut completely, and he woke up in his previous clone vessel on a small bed. He was at the same Indian air-force secret base as Rigasur. He immediately got up, opened the door, and rushed out.

New Hastinapur, Capital city of India

It was evening, and the sun had settled beyond the horizon. A slight mist was settling over the city's skyline, further dimming the fading pink hue in the sky.

Thousands of residents were gathering on the roads, on their terraces, and the balconies, all gazing up at the sky. A small part of the otherwise clouded sky was lit with a bright light. They could see a glowing speck thousands of kilometers up in the air.

Mobile phones, hand-held, and drone cameras were out. Frantic chat room discussions and frenzied social media live sessions swept through the internet. News stations switched programming; military control rooms were blaring with alarms. No one knew what the speck was, but one thing was clear: it was speeding towards the city.

A similar situation was occurring in NYC, though due to the time of day, fewer people noticed the ball of fire up in the sky. UFO alarms were triggered, and armed forces were put on high alert.

1:11…10…09…

Back at the control room, Rig was trying to establish a connection with Pri but was failing. The meltdown of the virtual reality had likely severed their server connection.

His attention was broken by a door slamming open behind him as Tej stormed in. "Where is Pri? Can you find her?"

"I was going to ask you the same question," Rigasur spoke over his shoulder and went back to studying the message board in front of him. "She is not responding to my messages."

"She said she has some unfinished task, asked me to leave."

"Yes, a critical task. She can control and stop the Brahm-Astras."

"What? How's that even possible?"

"That's the exact reason I asked Venkat to start firing the EMPs. I knew once the kids were out of the equation, you'd breach the doors, and Tamas's self-destruct trigger would activate. With Tamas gone, Pri will take over the system, and with that, the control of the weapons."

Tej stood motionless. Too much was happening too soon. A large digital clock on the wall showed a reverse countdown.

0:47...46...45...

"Forty-five seconds more, and this world will change forever." Rigasur pressed a few buttons on his keyboard, and two small windows opened on his laptop screen, showing the skyline of New Hastinapur and New York. A bright ball of fire was seen racing towards downward on New Hastinapur. The NYC skyline bore the same picture of doom.

"Come on, Pri, we are running out of time." Rigasur was using a fidget spinner in one hand and squeezing a stress ball with the other.

A monitor on each screen was also showing the speed of each of the balls of fire as measured by spectral instruments. The speed was slowly increasing as the Brahm-Astras descended.

0:21...19...18...

In New Hastinapur, the speck was not a mere dot anymore, but an illuminated ball of fire racing towards the city center. Though it was still hundreds of kilometers above, the light emanating from it was so bright that it was not possible to look at it with the naked eye. Some who tried to look at it were temporarily blinded or passed out. With the scathing glow came fiery heat.

The ground temperature had risen by five degrees Celsius. Glass windows on the top of few skyscrapers had started melting. Mega trash dumps throughout the city were experiencing massive fires. Vehicles on the road came to a standstill. Air-travel in and out of the city was temporarily suspended, and multiple flights coming into the city were urgently diverted.

Rigasur sat glued to his screen, mumbling something, when his lips came to a standstill. His whole body came to a standstill as if he was a mannequin made of wax. Something was happening. The Brahm-Astra speeds being displayed on the laptop screen were rapidly flickering. The charts first flattened out, then started decreasing.

"Yes!" Rigasur banged the table, startling Tej, who was sitting in the chair next to him.

"What?"

"She did it. Your daughter fucking did it." Rigasur got up and hugged Tej, squeezing him.

Tej was half relieved, half confused, and hugged Rigasur back.

Rigasur let Tej go. "If this control room were full of people, you would have heard thunderous applause, like in the movies. But unfortunately, we had to keep this situation discreet. I'm the only one rejoicing." Rigasur got back to the monitor and zoomed on the fireballs. They were slowing down, as well as changing their trajectory.

They took a parabolic U-turn a few kilometers above the ground and started to speed up back into the atmosphere, away from the cities.

"Why did she not bring them to a complete halt?" Tej asked, like a kid who had just witnessed a magic show.

"These ancient weapons are tricky to handle. Moving at such super-sonic speeds, it's impossible to slow them down in time. Changing their trajectory and directing them elsewhere is the best thing she could do."

"Directing them where?"

"Somewhere into deep space, away from the Earth. The planet is safe."

"Okay, and where is she?"

Rigasur paused and looked at Tej. "That, I don't know."

Inside the Arobaini castle, the dolphin stood at the edge of the oval tank, letting out a sad noise. A dark neurotoxic liquid was slowly diffusing into the tank, and the animal could smell it.

Tamas sat at one corner of the hall, its back balanced against the wall. The blue light in its eyes blinked a few times until it faded out.

Two miles away from Arobaini, three US Airforce choppers welcomed Brigadier Venkat and his team. Squadron leader Mireya Rivanchez saluted the brigadier. "General Griffin sends his regards, sir."

Venkat nodded and smiled.

Mireya walked with him to the chopper, "Sir, we will take you to USS Mariela, where you all will get the medical aid you need. After that, we will arrange travel for you back to your base at your convenience. Do you have all the soldiers and hostages accounted for?"

"Yes, all hostages are safe."

"After we leave, we have two F-536s fighters coming in."

Venkat lifted his left eyebrow. "To do what?"

"To turn that into ashes." Mireya pointed towards Arobaini.

"Fair enough." Venkat took a deep breath and hopped onto the chopper. "I'd need to make a call on the way."

Back in the control room, Tej sat in a chair with his hands covering his face. A thousand thoughts were going through his mind.

Rigasur had just opened a fresh bottle of twenty-five-year-old whiskey and was dropping ice-cubes in a fancy glass. "Tej, are you sure you don't want this elixir?"

Tej shot back, "No, Rig, my daughter is missing. So, forgive me for not celebrating yet."

Rigasur paid no attention and started pouring the whiskey. The laptop buzzed with an internet call. Rigasur pressed a button and picked up.

"Hey Rig, we did it!" Venkat's joyful voice filled the room.

"Cheers to that, Brigadier," Rigasur chuckled.

"Is Tej there? Around you?"

"Yes, he is here, sulking."

"Someone wants to talk to him."

Tej stood up and walked to the laptop. "Who is that?"

"Dad, it's me."

Tears rolled down Tej's cheeks. "Pri, you…how?"

"The brigadier got my vessel out. And after I was done doing what I had to do, I came back. I will see you very soon."

Tej let out a deep breath. Several million tons of weight were lifted off his shoulders.

"Still don't want this?" Rigasur dangled the glass in front of him.

Tej let out a laugh. "Why not? Now I can celebrate." He sat back on his chair and sank into it. Finally, it was all over.

A few hours later, a secret airstrip

A US military plane had just landed, and an operator was helping the pilot align it to a parking bay.

Tej was early waiting to get one glimpse of Pri, to make sure she was all right. Next to him stood Rigasur, smoking a cigar and coolly tapping his foot. Alongside them, a team of medics waited with their supplies.

As the plane's back-ramp opened up, Venkat jogged out and waved to Tej and Rigasur, who waved in return. Following him was a group of super-soldiers who marched right across them.

Venkat signaled the medical team to go inside the plane and attend to the wounded.

Tej gulped. He couldn't see Pri anywhere in the crowd.

Two of the medical staff finally came out with a stretcher following them, neatly floating in the air. Pri lay on it with her eyes closed.

Tej ran to her and took her hand in his. She opened her eyes and smiled. The medics gave them some space and stood at a distance.

Her face was covered with dust, blood, and bruises, but her smile melted his heart.

He caressed her forehead softly. "I thought I'd lost you, kiddo."

"You didn't. I was always going to come back."

Tej held his tears in. "You wanted to save the world on your own. You did it."

"No, Dad, we did it together."

Tej took her hand in his, and tears rolled down his cheeks.

16th June 2080, Miami Beach Florida

It was a clean night devoid of clouds, and people had gathered in large numbers to witness the spectacle of the century: a meteorite shower. Astronomers and enthusiasts were setting up telescopes and observation stations.

The asteroid NEA-511, which was "miraculously" broken up by Jupiter's gravity, was no longer on collision course with Earth. However, its fragments were going to fly by close to the planet, giving everyone a beautiful display. A very few people knew what had transpired behind the scenes, and how an ancient weapon took out a colossal asteroid.

Tej, Pri, and Rigasur had slipped among the crowd and were roaming around with cocktail glasses in their hands.

Pri was getting irritated listening to Tej and Rigasur's stories. She could no longer hold herself back. "What the hell are we doing here? The asteroid was destroyed by the Brahm-Astra, we saved the world, averted Doomsday, and watered down Tamas's evil plan. End of story. Do we need to see this meteorite shower?"

"Yeah, I think I'm getting bored too." Rigasur took a large gulp from his glass.

"What would you do now, Rig?" Tej slowed the pace of his walk.

All three of them stopped and sat on the sand facing each other as they continued talking.

"I think I'll take the long-pending vacation you interrupted to fight these evil villains. What about you?"

"My time is now devoted to Pri unless she wants to devote her time to someone else?" Tej eyed her and laughed.

"Let's not talk about that," Pri changed the topic. "I wanted to ask you something. Rig, how did you make that call, asking Venkat to act? Everything could have fallen apart."

"What can I say? I have a few talents which no one else has." Rig took another big gulp of cocktail

"Oh, come on. Be out with it."

Rigasur paused, then spoke. "All that time, Tamas was telling us how he was planning to destroy the world. But he never did that. What struck me was that he never wanted to cause an apocalypse in the first place. He only wanted to threaten the world with a weapon and bring powerful nations to their knees."

"And asteroid was that weapon?"

"No, the asteroid was a one-time uncontrollable warhead; that wouldn't have worked. He needed a catastrophic weapon that he could control. Plus, he also wanted us time demons out of the way. Turning an asteroid towards Earth solved both his problems. He pushed us to the corner by aiming an asteroid at us and suppressing any human attempts to counter it. He gave us the toughest challenge we could ever face, a situation so complex, it threw us off balance."

"That he did." Tej took a sip.

"And in our efforts to contain this tough situation, we brought into the world *Brahm-Astra*, a world-ending weapon which he could control. When I understood this, it struck me that he would have built some kind of control mechanism in the Brahm-Astra versions which he developed. Then it was only a matter of playing a bold game. I knew once Tamas was destructed, Pri would get hold of the system and could control the weapons. It was a close call."

"You are brilliant, Rig." Tej smiled.

Rig looked at Pri.

"What? Don't expect any compliments from me. Anyways I'll be heading out now."

Rigasur shrugged and got back to his drink.

"But I have to confess something before I leave."

Rigasur and Tej listened intently. They hadn't known Pri to open up easily.

Pri kept her drink aside and chewed her lower lip. "I can't take all the credit for stopping this apocalypse. When I was inside Tamas's mainframe, all my attempts to control these Brahm-Astra arrows were futile. I may have controlled one of them, but not both. Their terminal velocity was so extreme, I was failing."

"Then?"

"Then I felt a sudden burst of energy. I saw blue flames all around me. As if my powers were enhanced a thousand times. And then turning the weapons around was a piece of cake."

"Larem?" Tej was half-smiling.

Pri nodded. "She saved the world."

"No, kiddo, you did. You saved the world." Tej touched her cheek softly. "And remember, Larem is just an ocean; we are the sailors."

Pri chuckled. "Did she say the same words to you? She said that to me so many times."

Tej was smiling and nodding.

"Okay, you boys enjoy yourselves, see you later." Pri got up and walked away.

Tej and Rigasur looked at the sky as they heard the crowd cheering. The meteorite shower was about to begin.

THE END

ABOUT THE AUTHOR

Varun Sayal is a science fiction author who has built considerable repute in the writing world within a short period. His science fiction works, such as *Time Crawlers* and *Demons of Time*, have been phenomenal hits on Amazon, with five hundred positive reviews on Amazon and other platforms.

www.ingramcontent.com/pod-product-compliance
Lightning Source LLC
LaVergne TN
LVHW091634070526
838199LV00044B/1065